She'd had more expert lovers, men more practiced in the ways of arousing a woman, but what
Julie hadn't had before was a comfortable lover,
and Noah was just that. He wasn't trying to
overwhelm her with passion, nor was he setting
forth a bag of tricks with which to awe her.
Instead, they seemed to meld together as
naturally as an act of nature, as if all prior lovers
had been practice for the moment when she'd
meet Noah and every component would fit
together perfectly.

Julie could never imagine any other man ever
suiting her so well. Noah's kisses were seductive
without being sloppy. His hands moved with a
swift sureness over her body, not intent on
discovering new erogenous zones, but instead,
concentrating on the tried and true....

Dear Reader,

We're so proud to bring you Harlequin Intrigue. These books blend adventure and excitement with the compelling love stories you've come to associate with Harlequin.

This series is unique; it combines contemporary themes with the fast-paced action of a good old-fashioned page turner. You'll identify with these realistic heroines and their daring spirit as they seek the answers, flirting with both danger and passion along the way.

We hope you'll enjoy these new books, and look forward to your comments and suggestions.

The Editors
Harlequin Intrigue
919 Third Avenue
New York, N.Y. 10022

MISTAKEN IDENTITY

BEVERLY SOMMERS

Harlequin Books

TORONTO • NEW YORK • LONDON
AMSTERDAM • PARIS • SYDNEY • HAMBURG
STOCKHOLM • ATHENS • TOKYO • MILAN

Harlequin Intrigue edition published August 1984

ISBN 0-373-22003-0

Chapter One

She was never cut out to be a spy.

She was afraid of guns, disliked loud noises, scruffy-looking men who looked like budding revolutionaries, camping out, having to wear dirty clothes. The list was endless. She had never been a campus radical, belonged to no militant organizations, and subscribed to the *Wall Street Journal*. All of which made Julie an anomaly in her family.

Her father was John Domino, the one who does those special news reports for CBS. At one time he had been a war correspondent, quite a famous one, but he gave it up when he met her mother and they got married. He happened to meet her at the one dull period of history—his words, not Julie's—when there didn't happen to be a war around to cover. She guessed he married out of boredom. He found, however, that life with her mother was never boring.

Julie's mother was Ardith Domino, the ACLU lawyer one always reads about in the newspapers. For a long time Julie's mother was frustrated in her desire to be an active radical. Born in Norway, she was too young to be a part of the resistance during the Second World War. In college and law school in the fifties, she missed out on the radicalization of the campuses in the sixties. The women's movement appeared just in time to provide her with a cause, and she embraced it as firmly as she had ever embraced her children.

Julie was the middle child. Her older sister, Emery —she had her name legally changed from Emily, which she didn't feel suited her—was the champion of every downtrodden people on earth. She was a part of every protest march, every demonstration, her silvery-blond head standing out like a beacon amongst the dark heads of the Nicaraguan students or the South Africans or the Cambodians. Emery made a living filming documentaries and had a penchant for poignant dramas concerning revolutionaries and others of their ilk.

Julie's younger brother, Wally, still in graduate school, was into danger and adventure, which meant that he was, at that time, climbing mountains in the French Alps, his idea of a terrific summer vacation.

The evening when it all began Julie was anticipating nothing more adventurous than a stroll through Washington Square Park after dinner. Teaching economics for New York University made her eligible for housing in Greenwich Village as the university owned much of the real estate in the area. She had been provided with a small apartment which looked out on the park. Being just the right size for one person, it suited her perfectly. She loved living alone, the quiet best of all. That and the privacy. Coming from a noisy, gregarious family, she cherished both.

The humming of the air conditioner drowned out the sounds from the park across the street. Julie had two lamb chops cooking slowly in the broiler, a just-mixed salad chilling in the refrigerator, and her radio turned low to a classical station. She had been running around the city all day shopping and her feet were tired. She was just about to put them up and relax with one of the paperback Regencies she had purchased at Dalton's that afternoon when the telephone rang.

She disliked telephones.

They seemed to her to be the most insidious form of invasion of privacy ever invented. To somewhat circumvent this invasion of privacy she had installed a telephone answering machine that monitored her calls, which it was doing at this moment.

"Darling? I know you're there; I can sense it. Pick it up like a good girl, Julie—"

It was her mother. With a sigh, Julie picked up the phone and said hello.

"Sweetie, grab a taxi and get over here at once. We have a family emergency." Her mother sounded harried, but that was nothing unusual.

"I'll take a subway," Julie started to say, but her mother had already hung up. Julie tried to remember a telephone conversation where her mother had said either hello or good-bye, but couldn't remember any. Standard greetings were not her style.

She also never exaggerated: A family emergency would be just that. And there was no use speculating what kind of emergency it would be. In her family it could be anything.

She turned off the oven, set the air conditioner on

low, and left the apartment. It was still rush hour and she knew the Seventh Avenue subway would be quicker than trying to find a taxi. Anyway, she liked subways. She was an inveterate people watcher and subways satisfied this habit. There were usually as many people reading newspapers in Spanish as there were in English, and papers printed in Chinese, Greek, and Yiddish were almost as common. But just about all the commuters read some kind of paper, which made it easier for people watchers. People engrossed in reading seldom notice they're being watched.

The subway was too crowded at first to do anything but stare at the newspaper being held a scant two inches from her nose by a man crowded in front of her. The morning's headline about a hijacking had been replaced by one announcing a record-breaking number of bank robberies committed in the city that day. Before she got off, however, the crowd had thinned out and she had been able to compose life stories for several of the passengers. The most interesting was an extremely nervous older woman who was starting to look frayed around the edges. It was just little things—a run in her stocking, a button missing off her nylon blouse, makeup imperfectly applied. She seemed to be a potential shopping bag lady and that got Julie wondering whether there was a definite transition period one went through or whether it happened more abruptly. She often wondered whether at some point in her life *she* would somehow turn into a shopping bag lady without ever knowing quite how it happened.

Julie was still thinking about it when she got off at Seventy-second Street and walked west to Riverside Drive. One of her mother's law clerks opened the door, then disappeared into the recesses of the apartment. She hadn't been there in several months, and, looking around, she realized her entire apartment would fit into one corner of the gigantic living room.

Her mother came into the room looking tired but beautiful. She was barefoot and dressed in running shorts and a T-shirt which proclaimed God was a woman. Her straight blond hair was escaping from a knot and she attempted to smooth it with her fingers as she stood in front of Julie, her eyes showing concern.

"I know you're enjoying your self-imposed reclusiveness, Julie, but you must fly to Athens tonight."

Athens. She vaguely remembered her sister saying something to her about filming in Greece that summer. "Is it Emery?"

Her mother nodded and pulled her over to the couch. "She's disappeared. Some young man who's helping her with the film—I wrote his name down for you—called me earlier. He hasn't seen her since yesterday morning and says she hasn't been back to her apartment."

Knowing Emery, Julie didn't understand her mother's concern. "But that's just like her and it's only been a day. Anyway, Greece is such a safe place—not like some she's been to." Chad, for one, came to mind.

"You know I'm not the nervous mother, Julie, but the man seemed genuinely worried. Just because the colonels are no longer in power doesn't mean it isn't still something of a police state over there. He said she had missed two appointments he had difficulty setting up for her with former leaders of the underground. Also, he's a former resistance leader himself, and if *he* takes it seriously . . ."

She wondered why her mother wanted her to go. "Is Dad still in Japan?"

Her mother smiled. "Yes, I talked with him last night. The Japanese have offered him his own television show."

"He's not—"

"No, of course not. Although he's enjoying himself immensely there." She gave Julie an amused look. "You're wondering why I'm asking you to go, aren't you? Well, aside from the fact your father is in Japan, Wally is in France and inaccessible by phone, and I'm in the middle of a case, you're the logical one."

"Not by *my* logic. I would think I'd be the least likely."

She regarded Julie thoughtfully as she fitted a cigarette into a long, ebony holder. "I'd never send Wally or Emery on a mission of this kind. They'd get caught up in their own adventures and quite forget the reasons for going. But you're calm and practical and, it's an old-fashioned word, but steadfast comes to mind. And anyway, Julie, you could do with a vacation and Greece is charming." This last part was said with a smile.

The entire time they had been talking the telephones had been ringing, her mother's clerks and secretary had been in and out and confusion was the order of the day. Julie could hear Elton John, whom her mother adored, being played on one of the stereos; the news was on the TV, and, Charlie, Julie's favorite of the cats, was chasing a fly around the room with an absolute disregard for any furniture or lamps that might be in his way. Julie thought he missed her and was showing off for her benefit.

Her mother left the room and returned with a canvas attaché case with the word BRIEF stenciled on one side. "I assume your passport is up-to-date?"

Julie nodded and looked down at the case her mother had set on her lap.

"I had my secretary take care of everything. You're booked on the ten o'clock flight to Athens, Olympic Airlines. I wrote the flight number down for you. Also, the address of Emery's apartment and the name of the young man who called are in the case. You might as well use her apartment while you're there. I put in five hundred dollars just in case—there won't be time for you to get traveler's checks."

"I doubt whether I'll need that much money. And I've got American Express," Julie pointed out.

"Probably you won't, but take it anyway. Don't put it in your purse, though—hide some on your person."

Julie wondered how she was supposed to hide money on her person in thin summer clothes.

A gleam came into her mother's eyes. "Put some in your bra, Julie. That antiquated device ought to serve *some* useful purpose."

Julie got up, refusing to get drawn into their long-standing argument. She had already taken note of her mother's free form beneath the T-shirt she was wearing. At the moment she wanted to get home and pack. Rushing at the last minute was something Julie liked to avoid.

Her mother gave her a hug at the door. "I knew I could count on you, Julie. And listen, darling, when you get everything straightened out, stay on and have yourself a holiday. On me."

"Sure, Mom," she said, giving her a kiss. She'd been having a vacation all summer and was now looking forward to getting back to teaching. She had planned on spending the rest of the summer preparing her courses for the fall term. But she really didn't think it would take long to locate Emery. Chances were that Emery would be back at her apartment in Athens by the time Julie arrived there.

She got home with forty minutes to spare before having to leave for the airport. She reluctantly threw out the lamb chops, afraid to refreeze them half-cooked, but ate the salad she had already prepared. Knowing the odd ways of airlines she would probably be served dinner en route.

She packed light, taking only what she thought was absolutely necessary. She took two changes of clothing, some underwear and a pair of summer pajamas. And, of course, her hair dryer that worked on dual voltage. To her that hair dryer was a necessity. She and Emery had inherited their mother's light colored hair, but they had also inherited their father's unruly curls. Emery had always let her hair curl naturally around her head in a halo effect, which was fine if one wanted to stand out in a crowd, but Julie didn't. She had learned to straighten hers with a brush attachment on her dryer. And unless the humidity was very high or she got caught in the rain without an umbrella, she managed to keep her hair looking neat. As befitted a scholar. Or teacher.

Julie found her passport and transferred the money and information her mother had given her into a canvas handbag. Her bra remained unpadded. She changed into a khaki-colored cotton jumpsuit that zipped up the front, wound a double belt around her waist, and wore leather sandals with thick crepe soles that were comfortable for walking.

Before leaving she got the trash together to take out, made sure the oven was turned off, watered her plants and unplugged the air conditioner. She slipped three of the paperback novels into her handbag, then locked all four locks on her door. Emery called her a fussy person; Julie called it being well-organized.

She thought she would adore traveling if there weren't airplanes, airports, customs, and the exchange of money to contend with. If she could just miraculously be in another country without any hassle, travel would be heaven. Since she couldn't, it wasn't.

Efficiency didn't seem to be a byword for the Greeks. Olympic Airlines, assuming incorrectly that she wished to stay up all night watching a film, screened one for their viewing pleasure. They neglected, however, to pack the headsets. Having no desire to watch a silent movie, Julie got a blanket and pillow from the overhead rack, turned off her light, adjusted her seat to recline as much as possible, and tried to think positively. *I will sleep, I will sleep,* she repeated to herself, knowing full well she was never able to sleep on airplanes. Or on boats, trains, or busses. Or in the backseats of cars. In fact practically anywhere except in her own bed.

"Could I buy you a drink?" The balding business-man beside her was heard from.

"No thank you." She wanted to arrive in Athens sober. She tucked the blanket around her more snug-ly, turned away from him and tried to make her mind a blank. And, since she was trying to make it a blank, all sorts of jumbled thoughts began to crowd in.

"Sure you wouldn't like something? It's a long flight."

"No, thank you, I'm trying to sleep." Which should have been obvious to him.

A little later. "Can't I change your mind? I hate drinking alone."

He wasn't alone; most of the plane was drinking along with him. "I'm sleeping."

"No you're not, you're just trying to sleep."

Julie finally gave in just to shut him up. And as it turned out, the drink put her right to sleep. Which she was grateful for later as it was the best night's sleep she was to have for some time.

She was awakened by a voice over the public ad-dress system speaking in several indistinguishable languages. The flight attendant handed her landing cards to fill out: name, occupation, reason for visit, amount of currency being brought in, etc. Julie looked out the window at unbelievably blue sky and water and started to feel the sense of excitement she always felt when arriving at a new place.

Stepping down onto the landing field was a shock. As a New Yorker she was used to heat, but the heat here was incredible. It must have been a hundred degrees, the sun undiluted in the cloudless sky. The light was surgical in its intensity, making all appear to be foreground, wordless and bright.

The terminal building was, if anything, even hotter and filled with masses of travelers. Having carried her one piece of luggage on board with her, she didn't have to contend with the conveyor but got right into the lengthy line to go through customs.

It looked as though it was going to be a long wait. There was a group of young people in front of her with backpacks settling down on the floor. She unzipped her jumpsuit a few inches from the top and put up a hand to smooth back her hair. It was too late; she could already feel it standing up around her head. If it curled up that fast in just a few minutes her dryer would probably be useless while in Greece.

Since her nylon bag was unsuitable for sitting on, she stood and looked around. Waiting in lines, particularly at airports, was an excellent opportunity for people watchers. And foreign airports were the most interesting of all. Most of the people in line appeared to be tourists. She heard snatches of French and German being spoken and tuned in to some Italian, the only language other than English in which she was fluent.

Julie was somewhat stymied in her attempt at peo-

ple watching as the airport seemed filled with Greek
men who were female watchers, and several of them
seemed to be watching her. She was reminded of Italy, another country where the men were openly ap-
preciative of women. But she sensed that Greece was
also similar to Italy in that it wasn't a good idea to let
the men catch you watching them unless you were interested in striking up an instant friendship. Or something more than friendship.

But having nothing else to do, she went on observ-
ing, albeit in a surreptitious manner. As her eyes
moved around, trying not to pause too long on
anyone, she couldn't help noticing that one man was
watching her in a manner that bordered on outright
rudeness. He didn't seem to let her out of his sight
for a second, and since she was obviously not going
anywhere for some time, this seemed rather strange.
What was even more strange, he didn't appear to be
Greek. Nor was he watching her the way a man normally observes a woman. He didn't look interested in
her at all and even when she caught his eye he did
nothing more than continue his surveillance. Not a
smile, not a wink—nothing!

Very curious behavior indeed.

Julie looked around on the off chance she was
standing in front of a chart showing arrivals and
departures or something else that might have caught
his attention, but there was nothing behind her. She
glanced at him again: His eyes were still on her. *Well,
two can play at that game,* she thought, keeping her
eyes on him while she noted his appearance. He was
an attractive man, probably in his early thirties, with

light brown curly hair and mustache and eyes that could be seen to be blue even at a distance. He wore a light blue sport shirt, open at the neck, and tan trousers, and carried a jacket over one arm. He didn't appear to notice that she was staring back at him, and she began to think he was perhaps just staring into space and she happened to be occupying that space. She glanced to the right of him and saw another man who appeared to be watching the man who was watching her. At that point she decided she was becoming paranoid and busied herself with getting her passport out of her bag.

That bit of business took about one minute and then she was left with nothing to do once more. She glanced up again at the second man who was still watching the first. He appeared older than the other man, probably late thirties, forty at the most. He had a rumpled appearance, just the way she felt after the long flight. If he had also just gotten off a plane, however, she couldn't imagine why he was hanging around the airport. Because that's all either of them seemed to be doing. He was larger than her watcher, almost a teddy bear of a man, although he didn't look fat, just substantial. His hair was an indiscriminate shade of brown, worn rather shaggy, either out of design or because he had a bad haircut. She couldn't see the color of his eyes as they were on her watcher. She glanced back at the other man—yes, she was still being watched.

At that point the line started to move and she struck up a conversation with the students ahead of her. For some reason the customs' officials seemed to get really ambitious then, because the line started moving along and as far as she could see no one was being detained at all.

When she was pretty close to the head of the line she saw her watcher pass quite near to her. He walked right up to the customs' officials and she saw him showing them something as they conversed. Then she watched him leave the terminal and decided he was probably some kind of airport security guard. Just because he didn't have darker hair didn't mean he wasn't Greek. Greeks come in various descriptions.

When she finally got to the head of the line she was asked to open her bag. She knew it was usually students who have a hard time getting through customs, but in this case the students in front of her had been waved right through and the officials seemed to be concentrating their attention on her. She unzipped her bag and spread it apart. It was small and she didn't think it would take them long to go through it.

One official immediately pounced on her hair dryer and handed it to the other, who promptly disappeared with it. She was about to lodge a mild protest when "teddy bear" appeared, spoke to the official in Greek, and was handed her passport. He looked at it, looked at her, shrugged, then spoke again to the official. At this point the second official returned with what was left of her hair dryer. She was sure all the parts were still there, but when placed on the counter in several pieces it no longer resembled a hair dryer in the least.

Having traveled a lot as a child with two dominant

parents, Julie wasn't usually intimidated by petty officials. She decided enough was enough.

"I'd like my hair dryer put back together before I leave," she informed the first official. "I don't happen to have tools with me and I'm going to need it."

Even as she was speaking the words "teddy bear" was putting the pieces back in her bag and zipping it up. He handed her her passport.

"I wouldn't worry about it," he told her. "Your hair will dry fast here in the heat."

"You're an American?" she asked him, surprised that he had anything to do with Greek customs.

He gave a slow smile that deepened the lines around his eyes, eyes that she now saw were a dark shade of gray. He had a nice face, the kind people would tend to confide in. "I'm with the State Department," he informed her. "We try to look out for our fellow countrymen."

He picked up her bag, took her arm, and started to lead her out of the airport. She wasn't satisfied, however, and stopped in her tracks.

"Why can't you get them to put my dryer back together? I don't understand why they took it apart in the first place. Surely they've seen hair dryers before."

He got her moving again by propelling her forward by her elbow. "It's not worth bothering about," he assured her. "If they did put it back together I could guarantee you it wouldn't work. Buy another one if you really need it—they're quite cheap here."

She stopped again. "Oh, forget it. Anyway, thanks for hurrying them up, if that's what you did."

She reached out to take her bag from him but he held on to it firmly.

"I'll just find you a taxi," he said, steering her out the glass doors and to a row of cabs that were lined up in front of the terminal building. He opened the door to one and thrust her bag inside. At that moment her watcher from the airport suddenly appeared out of one of the other taxis and came up to her.

"Taxi, lady?" he asked her in an accent she couldn't place. "Special rates to Athens."

Before she could answer, "teddy bear" had the man by the arm and was hustling him off down the sidewalk, both of them arguing in an unfamiliar language. She took the opportunity of getting into the taxi and giving the driver her sister's address, then watched with satisfaction out the back window the looks of surprise on the faces of both men as they realized she was escaping. She didn't know why one of them had been watching her and why a member of her State Department had been watching the other one, but not given to intrigue, she didn't want any part of it and was hoping that would be the last she saw of either of them.

Julie spent the twenty minute ride into Athens looking out the window. Usually in a foreign city she would try to read all the signs, but the Greek made no sense at all to her so she just enjoyed the sights. It didn't look particularly foreign. It was mostly low, modern apartment buildings and with the palm trees the whole place reminded her of the less desirable parts of Florida. But shortly after reaching what appeared to be the center of the city, the driver turned off down a narrow street and they seemed to be in a much older section.

It was a huddled uphill arrangement of irregular white buildings, the streets a series of mazes and archways. Laundry was hanging on balconies and in walled gardens and there was a sense of realized space, common objects, domestic life going on in the heated hush of midday. Stairways bent around houses, disappearing from her view, and the detailing light made textured pigment of the walls. She caught sight of a sea-green door, a handrail varnished to a nautical gloss, a cat slinking through the shadows of a doorway.

The driver pulled up in front of an old, narrow four-story building which housed a bakery on street level, and she got out. After paying the driver what seemed after New York to be almost nothing, he pulled off and she stood looking up at the building.

Even without being told she knew for a fact that her sister's apartment was the third floor front. Every apartment on the street save one had pots filled with geraniums set out on the balconies. Most of them also had chairs, tables and birdcages. Emery never stayed anywhere long enough to collect even a plant, let alone a pet. Julie wasn't worried about being locked out: Emery also never locked a door.

She walked up narrow wooden steps to the third floor and sure enough, the front apartment opened without benefit of key. It was a small apartment. One room with sleeping alcove, tiny kitchen and bathroom, and she saw signs of her sister everywhere. Sure signs of Emery were: no cooking utensils in the kitchen, but a bottle of wine in the refrigerator; a spare pair of Levi's and a couple of T-shirts in the closet, but no dresses; usually a mattress on the floor—in this case it was a cot, but the apartment probably came furnished; and no books anywhere. Any place Julie lived in for even one day would end up having at least a couple of books around, but Emery was more visually oriented, hence her interest in filmmaking.

Give me just one week, Julie was thinking, and I could turn the place into a charming home-away-from-home. It was hot and stuffy and she went over to open up the shuttered doors that led out to the balcony. She saw the Acropolis then for the first time. She thought the view of the park at home was nice, but it couldn't compare to this. Whatever else Athens lacked it more than made up for with the Acropolis, she thought, breathing in the sight.

She went out on the balcony for a closer look, vowing to walk up and see it for herself at the first opportunity. She didn't know what made her look down at the street before going back inside, but there, seated in a sidewalk café across the street, was her teddy bear from the airport. He didn't see her but appeared to be staring at something in front of her building. She leaned over the railing and looked down. Lounging in front of the bakery, a newspaper held in front of his face, was her watcher from the airport. She didn't know whether he thought he was blending into the scenery, but he looked pretty conspicuous to her, particularly since it appeared to be siesta time and the streets were deserted.

She was beginning to feel annoyed and thought of going down and confronting them both, demanding to be told the reason for their interest in her, but the thought of a cold shower and a change of clothes won out. Let the fools stay out there in the hot afternoon sun!

Chapter Two

The Greeks don't want you to forget you're in a foreign country. With this in mind, instead of a regular shower stall or a bathtub with shower, they place a shower head in the ceiling of the bathroom so that when you stand under it to take a shower, the entire bathroom takes one with you. A drain in the floor prevents you from floating away.

The water was more lukewarm than cold, but she felt refreshed as she stepped out of the bathroom. Towels had been provided, but she hadn't thought of removing them from the room first so they were too wet to be of any use after. She crossed the room dripping wet and found a cotton kimono in the closet and put it on over her wet body, then quickly unpacked her few things and hung them up. The only available mirror was steamed up in the bathroom so she didn't get a chance to see how badly her hair was frizzing at this point.

Julie was standing at the closet with her back to the front door when she heard it open. Her first thought was that Emery had returned and she had made the trip for nothing. But then she turned, just in time to see a strange man advancing toward her, a huge smile of relief on his face. She didn't have time to feel anything but surprise before he had her in his arms and was pulling her close.

"I thought I heard someone in here," he said to her before bestowing a sloppy kiss on her open mouth. Needless to say it was open from surprise, not in anticipation of a kiss coming its way.

It didn't last long. He drew back and gave her a quizzical look. "You're not Emery—Emery knows how to kiss," he said to her in an accusing way, but before she could feel properly insulted, he started to laugh. "You're Julie, the sister, am I correct? Yes, your mother said you'd be coming. What she didn't tell me was that you look enough like her to be her twin. Except that you're shorter. And maybe not as...uh...thin in some places."

"And younger," Julie pointed out, feeling she was getting the worst of the comparison. She wanted to ask him under what circumstances he felt free to just walk in without even a knock and kiss her sister like that, but on second thought she was afraid he'd tell her, and she thought Emery deserved *some* privacy. "Might I ask your name?" she inquired of him.

He held out his hand in the European fashion. "Heracles—Heracles Tadakis. I'm a good friend of your sister's; I've been helping her with the background for her film."

"Ah, the former resistance leader." Julie recalled what her mother had told her.

He laughed. "You'll find many former resistance leaders in Greece."

"And you're worried about Emery's disappearance?"

"Of course. She missed two important appointments, ones she was very anxious to keep."

He had the kind of good looks one expects to see in a Greek statue, and she was thinking that if she were Emery she wouldn't run out on him, let alone the two appointments. He was tall, with a lean, strong-looking body, and had the black curly hair and dark eyes she was partial to. Actually, he had the same kind of looks her father and brother had; she had always been disappointed she took after the Norwegian side of the family rather than the Italian. He also spoke excellent English with just enough of an accent to make him sound romantic. Unlike some others she had met since her arrival. Which reminded her of the two men outside, something she thought Heracles should be apprised of.

She told him about what had happened at the airport. "It just occurred to me that if *you* took me for Emery, perhaps those two men did, too, and maybe that would account for it. I certainly don't know why *I'd* be watched at the airport. Although one of them saw my passport, so he must know I'm not my sister, wouldn't you think?"

"And you say they're outside now?" Heracles asked, showing no surprise at what she had told him.

"Sure, come over and look." She went out on the balcony but he seemed to hang back. "They won't see you. One's too busy watching the other one, and the other one's too busy trying to look inconspicuous.''

He gave a chuckle and joined her. "Ummm. I know who they are, but I can't imagine what their interest would be in Emery. The one at the table is Colonel Majors. He's CIA.''

"He told me he was with the State Department.''

"Same thing. The other one, though, is with Mossad, and that doesn't make any sense at all.''

"What's Mossad?''

He turned back into the room. "Israeli secret police.''

She was confused. "But we're friends with Israel. Why would someone from the CIA be watching an Israeli?''

"I don't know. Nor do I know why either of them would be watching Emery.''

She gave a sigh of exasperation. "Then there's only one thing to do. Let's go down and ask them. Maybe they have to play at being spies, but I don't.'' She had the door open and was halfway out when his voice stopped her.

"Are you going out in the street dressed like that? We allow tourists a lot of leniency, but still. . .''

Julie could feel the flush covering her face as it dawned on her she had been wearing nothing but a kimono, and a wet one at that, since his arrival.

He seemed to sense her embarrassment. "I'll wait out in the hall while you change. Incidentally, I live right below you.''

Talk about feeling stupid! She couldn't believe she had been parading around the apartment in front of a total stranger wearing nothing more than a thin, slightly transparent, cotton wrap. And he must certainly have noticed that was all she was wearing when he took her in his arms. The only one in her family with any degree of modesty at all, and she had blown it.

She dressed quickly in a cotton blouse and pants, slipping into her sandals, then went out to join Heracles.

He grinned down at her. "Don't be embarrassed, I've seen Emery in a lot less."

"Yes, but you know Emery," she muttered, wondering how he could possibly have seen her in a lot less. Just a little less and she would have been stark naked.

As they came out into the street, the Mossad agent took one look at them and vanished around the corner.

"Watch our CIA friend while I go after him," said Heracles. "I know every inch of the Plaka, he won't get far." He also practically vanished around the corner into a narrow street and Julie turned in time to see the teddy bear getting quickly up from his table as though to pursue them.

She crossed the street and was at his table just as he was putting down some money. "I would really like to know why you've been following me," she began, and saw a look of amusement cross his face.

He glanced across the street, back at her, then seemed to come to a decision. "Would you care for some coffee? Maybe a lemonade?" he asked, pulling out a chair for her in a manner that only waiters seemed to do these days, and then not all that often.

She decided it would be just as sensible to confront him seated. "I'll have a lemonade, please."

He called out something to the waiter, then sat back down. "I haven't been following you."

"Very well, I'll reword that. I'd like to know why you've been following the Mossad agent who's been following me. I'd also like to know why he's been following me, if you happen to know that. I'm also curious as to why a CIA agent would be following a Mossad agent in the first place since it's my understanding we're on friendly terms with Israel." And what a long-winded speech; she felt like she'd been lecturing one of her classes.

He was looking amused again, one of his less appealing expressions. "Where on earth did you get the idea I'm a CIA agent?" All innocence now.

"Heracles told me you were."

"The average Greek assumes incorrectly that anyone connected with the embassy is some sort of spy."

"Heracles is not the average Greek," she countered. "He was one of the leaders of the resistance."

He nodded. "And as such would see CIA plots everywhere."

"And probably with good reason," she couldn't resist saying.

He lit a cigarette and took a leisurely sip of his coffee. "My dear Miss Domino, do I look like a spy to you?"

"My dear Colonel Majors," she said, thinking what a ridiculous name that was, "I must admit that you do. Not your person, no. You look too old, too rumpled, too out of shape. You have coffee stains on your tie, cigarette burns in your jacket, bloodshot eyes, and that's the worst haircut I've ever seen. In short, James Bond you're not! However, appearances aside, yes—I would take you for a spy. I find it hard to believe that the average State Department employee would keep another spy under strict surveillance unless he were himself a spy.''

She was out of breath when she finished speaking. She was certain he would take offense at her criticism of his appearance, but he merely laughed good-naturedly.

"You know, Miss Domino, you're pretty astute for—''

"A blonde?'' she cut in.

"That's not what I was going to say.''

"Pretty astute for a woman?'' she guessed.

He shook his head. "I wish you'd quit putting words in my mouth. What I was trying to say was you're pretty astute for someone not in the business.'' He paused a moment. "Or are you in the business? Is that why Yotav is following you?''

"If Yotav is the Mossad agent, I told you before I don't know why he's following me. Except that it's possible he thinks I'm my sister.''

"Your sister's a spy?''

She gave a sigh. "No, my sister's not a spy.'' She said this with more assurance than she felt, however. It was quite possible that being a spy would appeal to Emery. Although not for the CIA, she was sure.

He was smiling at her again. "You want to go dancing tonight?''

She couldn't believe she had heard him correctly. "Dancing?''

His expression relaxed and his smile was lazy. "At the rooftop of the Hilton. They have two orchestras and a fantastic view of the city."

"I didn't come here to dance, Colonel; I came to find my sister," she said, emphasizing every single word.

"Find her? Is she lost?"

She debated for a moment whether to tell him, but after all if you couldn't trust your own State Department...

"She seems to have disappeared."

He dropped the smile and began to look serious. "Why didn't your family notify the embassy here?"

"Well, you see, with Emery it could turn out to be almost anything, and I guess Mother was trying to avoid publicity—for Father's sake."

He was suddenly looking at her with interest for the first time. At least serious interest. "Wait a minute...Domino...your father's John Domino?"

She nodded.

"Hey, I know him! I always admired his work. We shared a few drinks once in Saigon. Why didn't he come over here? He knows his way around Athens— hell, around anywhere!"

"He's in Japan at the moment."

He raised a shaggy brow. "What about your mother?"

"She's in the middle of a case—she's an attorney."

He chuckled. "So they sent *you* over? A *kid*?"

Any comments made about her not looking her age did not go over very well with Julie. It was hard enough teaching at NYU where half the students looked older. "I happen to be twenty-nine," she informed him cooly.

"That old, huh? What are you, the private detective in the family?"

She was beginning to be annoyed by his flippant manner. "I'm an economist."

"You don't look like an economist," he said, his gray eyes taking on the gleam of mercury.

"You don't look like a spy," she shot back at him.

He laughed. "You sure you don't want to go dancing? Although I'm not sure your father would approve of me—not for his daughter, anyway."

"No one in my family would approve of anyone in the CIA," she informed him coldly, although that wasn't quite true. It was only her mother and Emery who would probably disapprove.

"Your father would approve. Maybe not of me, but of the CIA in general."

She wondered why he thought Father wouldn't approve of him, but was afraid if she asked he would take it as a sign of personal interest in him, of which she had none.

"Why don't I pick you up tonight—"

"Colonel!"

"You can call me Noah."

Noah? She'd never known anyone named Noah. It would be easy to remember, though—just think of teddy bears and then of Noah's ark . . .

"I don't want to call you Noah," she said, starting to lose her temper. "Colonel, I'm here to locate my sister, not to visit the rooftop of the Hilton."

He grinned. "Don't economists dance?"

"Not this one!" She got up, thinking she'd prefer to wait for Heracles in Emery's apartment. She was afraid if she stayed the colonel and she would come to blows.

He reached out and took a firm hold of her wrist. "Hey, you have Johnny's temper. Come on, sit down—I swear I won't mention dancing anymore."

Johnny? She had never heard anyone call her father Johnny. The colonel was wearing his confidable face again and she found herself doing as he said. "I generally don't have a temper at all," she told him, and this was true. She prided herself on being the only calm member of a volatile family. But there was something about this Noah Majors that she found provoking. When he wasn't asking her to go dancing, he was treating her like a child.

He seemed to sense she had calmed down and released her wrist. "So, Julia, tell me about your sister."

"Julia?"

"That was the name on your passport."

"I've always been called Julie." She gave him a sweet smile. "But you can call me *Ms* Domino."

"If you don't start showing some respect to a member of your country's State Department, I'll call you a—"

"Never mind," she interrupted him, trying not to laugh. Then she remembered she had nicknamed him teddy bear, and she did start to laugh.

He shook his head. "Well, whatever it is about your sister, it couldn't be too serious or you wouldn't be sitting here laughing."

"Buy me something stronger than a lemonade, Colonel, and I'll tell you all about it."

"How about an ouzo?"

"Fine."

The waiter brought her what looked like a small glass of water and a large glass of water. She took a sip from the large glass. It was water. She took a sip from the small glass and discovered that special sensation fire-eaters must experience. The colonel was enjoying her reaction.

"Ready to talk now?" he asked.

She wasn't sure her vocal chords were still functioning. She took a long drink from the large glass and gave it a try.

"She hasn't been seen since yesterday morning. Emery. My sister."

"What is she, a student?"

She shook her head. "No, she's two years older than me. She was over here filming a documentary."

"Of what?"

"I'm not quite sure. All I know is she had been meeting with former members of the resistance."

He looked perplexed. "That doesn't make sense."

"Oh, sure it does. Emery always films stuff like that, it's what interests her."

"I meant it doesn't make sense that Mossad would be interested in her."

"You mean you really don't know why that man is following me?" She took another sip of the ouzo, making sure he noticed she could manage it now without choking. His look was congratulatory.

"If I knew that, I wouldn't have to follow him."

"For a spy you're not much help."

Noah spread his arms in a helpless gesture. "I'm not a spy and you haven't told me much."

He was looking over her head. "Your friend is across the street trying to get your attention."

She looked around. "His name is Heracles," she told him, motioning to Heracles to come join them.

"I figured it was Adonis," he muttered, making her laugh again.

She could see Heracles shaking his head and motioning for her to join him instead.

She got up. "Thank you for the lemonade and the ouzo, Colonel." Not being as mannerly as she, he didn't get up.

"Wait a minute," he said, getting out a notepad and pen and writing something down. He ripped out a sheet and handed it to her. "Here, take my number. I'll do some checking on your sister for you. Call me later tonight and I'll let you know if I have anything. Better yet, meet me at the rooftop of the Hilton."

"You don't let anything interfere with your dancing, do you?" she asked him sarcastically.

He put on a sad face. "You know how it is when you're a spy. Death is always just around the corner, so you want to enjoy the few moments available to you." Then the corners of his mouth began to twitch as though even he couldn't swallow all the nonsense he was spouting.

She held out her hand and he took it. "I appreciate your looking into it and I will call you later. And Colonel..."

He began to look expectant.

". . . enjoy your few moments."

She could hear him laughing behind her as she crossed the street to join Heracles.

They went up to Heracles's apartment, the same floor plan as that of Emery's but more fully furnished. Particularly notable was a large bed that filled half the room. The rest of the space was taken up by books, a decorating feature after Julie's heart. She couldn't help wondering how much time her sister had spent in this apartment and how she always managed to find the most attractive man in any city she visited. Despite their similar looks, Emery had always been more successful than Julie when it came to attracting men. Julie felt she'd always been an underachiever in that area.

She told Heracles about her conversation with Colonel Majors while he prepared them cups of thick, Turkish coffee. She welcomed the drink as she was feeling the effects of the ouzo, which effects she had begun to feel as soon as she had got to her feet at the sidewalk café.

"You did better than I did," he told her with a wry smile. "I lost Yotav almost immediately."

"I thought you said you knew every inch of the Plaka?"

"It would appear that he does also."

She sat down on the floor with her coffee. The only other place to sit was on the bed and she didn't want the conversation with Heracles to become too intimate. "Tell me something," she asked him, "why would you get worried about my sister after only one day? She's been known to disappear for much longer stretches of time than that."

"A number of reasons," he said, propping up pillows behind his head as he stretched out on the bed. "She was supposed to meet me Tuesday afternoon to talk to some people who had made a special trip down from Solonika, people she wanted very much to interview. And last night was the Theodorakis concert."

All Julie knew about Theodorakis was his song "Zorba the Greek," and all she currently knew about Turkish coffee was that it tasted like regular coffee left in the pot for two weeks. She was sipping it to be polite but wished she had some water to wash it down.

"He was probably the best known of the resistance people and this was to be his first concert since his self-imposed exile. But in retrospect, the most important thing was that the last time I saw Emery she was on her way to the airport to do a filmed interview of Theodorakis as he landed in Athens. I waved her off in a taxi, and that's the last she was seen. I talked to Theo and she never showed up for the interview. All of this would have been enough to worry me, but I wouldn't have bothered your family about it. I would just had set things in motion to find her myself." He paused for a moment, then, "Would you like some more coffee?"

"No thanks," said Julie, who'd been hoping he wouldn't ask.

"Anyway, last night I heard that the police were also looking for her, and since she's not a citizen I thought your family should be apprised of the situation. In the case of foreigners, your own State Department can usually be more effective than the police.''

"Why would the police be looking for Emery?" she asked, wondering why her mother hadn't mentioned that aspect of the situation to her. It wouldn't have slipped her mind—nothing ever slipped her mother's sharp mind.

"No one's saying, only I did find out it's not because of anything she's done. At least nothing illegal." He shrugged expressively. "Although what *you* can do about any of it I just don't know. I have a whole network of people trying to find out what's happened."

Julie shifted her position on the floor, trying to get comfortable. "So the last time you saw her she was headed for the airport. What time was that?"

"About ten. The plane was due in at eleven, so that gave her plenty of time to get out there and set up. As it turned out, however, it was delayed because of the hijacking. Oh, hell!" he said, banging his head back against the wall in frustration. "Why didn't I make the connection before this?"

"You mean the hijacking?"

"It must have something to do with that. Of course!"

While the idea of it might appeal to her adventurous spirit, she just couldn't see Emery getting mixed up with hijackers, if for no other reason than she wouldn't want to embarrass their father. "Emery would never have been party to a hijacking," she told

Heracles, trying to sound positive in the face of doubts.

"No, of course not," he said, sounding even less positive, "but it must be connected. Maybe she saw something she wasn't supposed to see."

Julie didn't like the sound of that. Seeing something you weren't supposed to see could lead to a lot of trouble. Maybe even danger. She set her cup on the floor and stood up, feeling a little stiff from sitting on the hard surface. She glanced at the titles of the books in the shelves, but they all looked Greek to her. "A lot of people must have seen the hijacking, particularly with all the tourists at the airport this time of year," she reasoned.

He nodded. "Yes. The newspaper reports cited many witnesses."

"Who did the hijacking, Heracles?"

"Witnesses seemed to be in agreement that they were Arabs. There were about a half dozen of them, I believe, all wearing kaffiyehs on their heads. What made this a little different than the usual hijacking was that so far no group has taken the credit."

"That doesn't make any sense," she said. "I thought the whole point of hijackings was for the resultant publicity."

He nodded. "Usually several groups jump in to take credit."

"However," she said, and saw that she had his attention, "that would explain why Mossad is interested."

His head was going up and down and his eyes

gleamed. "Of course. And it was an El Al plane that was hijacked!"

Julie wished now that she had read the newspaper reports of the hijacking. "Where did the plane finally land?"

"That's even more strange. No country has reported its landing." He got off the bed, upsetting his coffee in his agitation. He didn't bother with it, so she picked up both cups and took them over to the kitchen sink.

"I think I should go out to the airport and do some questioning myself," he said to her.

"I'll go with you."

He shook his head. "You look too much like Emery. If they gave you a hard time there before, it's better if I go alone." He glanced at the digital watch strapped to his wrist. "I'll meet you back at Emery's apartment at eight."

She felt frustrated not having anything definite to do for the next few hours, but she was also very hungry and it would give her a chance to see the Acropolis. And she really wasn't in a hurry to see the airport again.

She looked out his window to see if perhaps her two watchers were back on the job. They weren't, but she had to chuckle at the thought of how quickly she had developed clandestine paranoia.

When Heracles left she got a sponge from the kitchen and cleaned up the spilled coffee, then straightened out the spread on his bed before going upstairs to collect her handbag.

She didn't like the idea of carrying around five

hundred dollars in cash, something she'd never do in New York, but she liked leaving it in an unlocked apartment even less. And since she had no key, it would have to remain unlocked.

She looked around for a hiding place but could find nothing suitable and decided she'd just have to be careful. Taking a look in the bathroom mirror she saw that her hair was in its halo effect and there wasn't anything she could do about it. No dryer, lots of humidity—a bad combination. Giving it up as a lost cause, she left the building and headed in the general direction of the Acropolis.

The buildings were all small and very old with red-tiled roofs and flowered vines hanging over the doorways, the streets narrow in twisting mazelike patterns, filled with a jumble of little shops and tavernas. Everywhere she turned there seemed to be steps, mostly leading up. Shops were beginning to open up and brightly colored caftans were being hung outside their doors.

As the street rose, it turned into nothing more than a dirt path. A flea-bitten cat stared out at her from the doorway of a shop, then scuttled into an alleyway. Somebody was singing strange music in a nearby street. On top of an artisan's shop, a girl with brown hair and brown lips opened a shutter and looked down at her. An old woman came out of a house and poured water from a pail onto the path. They were all slum houses built on the slopes, everything of stone. Julie couldn't see the Acropolis now, but knew from the steep rise that she was on its foundation.

She continued upwards and counterclockwise, the

houses above obscuring the view. She was getting hot and tired as she mounted rickety, crooked stone steps that led to more dirt paths, and then to other flights of stairs. Grass and bitter clumps of acacia trees occasionally spread some shade.

At last she came to a wide clearing and above her was the fortification on which stood the temples. Below lay the Agora strewn with the rubbish of columns, statues, and pieces of uncovered floors with stones stacked in piles. A resurrection of an ancient stoa stood housing a new museum.

The roadway led straight to St. Paul's rock and she climbed upon it, feeling a hot and gentle breeze brush against her. Below was Athens, spread out to the sea, a reflecting strip of blue. The city stretched out, a million boxy gray houses, each distinguishable and separate in the light.

Across from her sat the Parthenon, lucid and white against the blue infinity of the sky, looking shockingly familiar to her. She'd had a picture of it in her head, built up by books, embroidered by pictures and postcards. Despite its familiarity, she was stunned by its beauty.

At the foot of the Acropolis tourists were standing with their heads cocked back to take in the beauty of the Parthenon. Julie wasn't content to see it from a distance and kept going. On top the Acropolis was all rock. Not a bloom or a bud of grass. It was huge: rock, marble, lime, an abstract field of shapes, all white and black, except for the panorama of blue sky and the fields of cedars and city buildings below. The wind swept through the columns and she felt as though she were on top of the world.

Only the insistent grumbling of her stomach finally got her moving away from the sight. She would eat now, but she vowed she'd be back for another look before she left Athens.

Julie saw two young tourist police standing at a gate and decided to ask them if there was a good restaurant nearby. The one she asked seemed delighted to use his English and was pointing in the direction of what he insisted was a superior restaurant, when his friend took something out of his pocket and passed it to him. From where she stood she could see that it was a photograph, and too late she noticed they were comparing her to the picture. She should have been smarter than to have called attention to herself to the authorities, knowing they were interested in Emery's whereabouts, but she still wasn't used to the intrigue she was caught up in.

She started to leave, but it was too late. The friendly policeman of a moment before was now detaining her and his flirtatious manner had been replaced with one of authority.

She tried to reason with them, telling them her name was Julie, even reaching into her bag to show them her passport. But it seemed they only had a picture to go by, not a name, and there was no arguing that she didn't look just like the picture they showed her, even the exact same head of white-blond curls.

Not given to making scenes in public, she followed the two officers to where their car was parked and hoped she would be able to clear up the misunderstanding in short order before she starved to death.

Chapter Three

It seemed incredible to Julie that she was meeting one attractive man after another, particularly in such a short space of time, although to be perfectly honest most of them showed interest only because they believed her to be her sister.

This one—maybe the Chief of Police of Athens, maybe just a police officer—was exceedingly handsome from the tips of silver at his temples right down to the well-polished toes of his shoes. Everything in between seemed perfectly placed. She sighed, wondering why the men in New York never looked this good to her.

Sitting in on the interrogation, if that's what it was, was Yotav, formally introduced to her as Yotav Eshkol. The name, however, wasn't of importance. What was was the fact that he held stubbornly to his belief she was Emery. He dismissed the evidence of her passport with a shrug, pointing out that any spy would carry more than one identity in case of emergency.

"Even if I were Emery, which I'm not," she said

to the chief, "from what I've heard she's done nothing illegal, so I'd like to know why I'm being detained."

The two men spoke at the same time, the chief assuring her she wasn't being detained, and Yotav asking her where she had heard that.

She ignored Yotav and got to her feet, her eyes on the handsome Greek. "Well, if I'm not being detained I'll just take my leave."

She heard Yotav chuckle, proving to her that even spies had a sense of humor.

"A few more questions please, if you don't mind," said the chief, and Julie sat back down in as ungracious manner as she could manage.

"What have you heard about your sister doing nothing illegal?" asked the chief, the word *sister* sounding dubious on his lips.

"I just heard you were looking for her but not for any crime she'd committed."

The chief seemed to pounce on this bit of information. "Who told you that?"

A pause. "I don't remember," said Julie, wondering when she had started lying to police. But they weren't her police and she'd certainly done nothing wrong. And she was now so hungry she was sure the two men could hear her complaining stomach.

"I could help her remember," said Yotav, and Julie had images of being slowly tortured in an effort to make her talk.

She looked over at him and despite his words couldn't gain any sense of danger to herself. He was just too cute to inspire fear. She didn't often think of grown men as cute but that's how he struck her. He was dressed casually at the moment in T-shirt and jeans and his hair had a nice curl to it, his rimless glasses he now wore making his blue eyes look almost luminous. The dimple in his chin didn't hurt, either.

"I will question her first," said the chief, which seemed to mean that Yotav would get his chance later. Cute as he was, Julie preferred eating to torture any day of the week.

"I must insist that you allow me to call my embassy," Julie said firmly. She was an American, wasn't she? Didn't that count for anything in this part of the world?

"I will notify your embassy," said the chief.

"I think not," said Julie. "As a matter of fact Colonel Majors is waiting to hear from me...." The sudden look of alarm in the chief's eyes stopped her. Another lie on her part, but this one seemed to hit the mark.

"Very well, I'll get the colonel on the line for you," the chief was saying, ignoring the look of outraged indignation on Yotav's face. Once more the inducement of foreign aid won out, thought Julie, but she wasn't complaining.

Yotav was pacing about the small office in an agitated manner while the chief placed the phone call, then handed the receiver to Julie. Sure enough she could detect Noah's voice on the other end. Much as she hated to place herself in the position of being rescued by him, no better idea had come to mind and at least this one had worked.

"This is Julie Domino, Colonel. The Greek police

seem to be detaining me for unknown reasons and your friend from Mossad is here waiting to get into the act.''

She heard a chuckle. "And you need saving? Is that it?"

"Something like that."

"Hang in there, I'll be right down."

"Couldn't you just talk to him on the phone?" She didn't feel like spending any more time in the office with two disbelieving adversaries.

"Not a chance. And the offer to go dancing is still open..." Julie waited to hear more but the line had been disconnected. The fool—joking about dancing at a time like this. It was food she required, not exercise.

Julie replaced the phone and remained standing. She might have to wait for Noah to arrive, but she didn't see why she had to wait in here. "Do you have a ladies' room I could use?" she asked politely, ignoring the furious looks she was getting from Yotav.

The chief looked nonplussed. "I'm afraid not..."

Of course not. Why would the Athens police think a ladies' room necessary since they obviously didn't think it necessary to hire women to begin with. And women brought in to be questioned were just made to suffer.

She decided to reword her request. "Do you have a bathroom I could be permitted to use?"

"Of course," said the chief, getting to his feet and preceding her to the door. He made a right turn in the hall and Julie followed him several yards, then waited while he peered inside to make sure it was vacant.

"I will personally stand guard outside," he assured her, and Julie slipped past him sideways through the door to come face to face with a urinal.

Which wouldn't do at all. She turned and saw with relief that there was also an enclosed toilet, and availed herself of it. She had thought to waste time trying to do something with her hair and maybe even applying some makeup, but neither the small room nor her purse contained a mirror. She spent a long time washing her hands, then left the room and followed the Greek back to his office.

Yotav was helping himself to the chief's phone when she entered the office, and the chief, after one glance at the Israeli, told Julie he'd be right back and then went off down the hall.

Julie sat down, then reached inside her handbag and retrieved one of her paperbacks, opening it to page one and determined to ignore the spy seated across from her.

Yotav slammed down the phone and broke her concentration. "Your government cooperates with mine," he informed her, his hands busily trying to straighten out his naturally curly hair. Julie knew from experience what a frustratingly impossible task this was.

"I had always thought so," said Julie, giving him the merest glance up from her book. "Since in this case, however, Colonel Majors claims not to have a clue what you're doing..." Her eyes went back down to read the words that didn't seem half as interesting as what was happening to her in real life. Which was a decided change. Usually any adventure in her life was acquired vicariously from books.

Yotav muttered something in a foreign tongue as Julie continued to ignore him. Then, "We'll find it, you know, whether you cooperate or not."

"Find what?"

He gave her a disbelieving look as though she should know exactly what the *what* was he was referring to. "You did not go unobserved." This was said in as threatening a way as could be managed by a man with a dimple in his chin and Julie almost laughed out loud.

Since he was intent on being mysterious, she decided to change the subject. "I'm aware I've not gone unobserved since the airport. What I can't understand is why."

Yotav answered this by laughing, and Noah chose that moment to enter the office, still looking rumpled, now looking as though he needed a shave as well as a haircut, but nonetheless looking to Julie like the Marines to the rescue.

"I'm glad to see you're keeping Yotav entertained," he said to her, bringing Yotav's laughter to a hasty conclusion.

Julie put her book back in her bag and stood up, waiting for Noah to get her released. Noah seemed in no hurry, though, and was engaging Yotav in a conversation that was no doubt Hebrew as it didn't make any sense to her at all. Of course it could be Greek, only why would they be speaking in Greek?

Noah seemed to be berating the man and yet at the same time Julie could sense a camaraderie between them and got the feeling they were either personal friends or had worked together at some time in the past. There was no doubt that they were not working together now, however, as Yotav said something that Julie could tell was uncomplimentary in any language before storming out of the office. Yes, storming. She wasn't sure she'd ever seen anyone actually storm out of a place before, but this was clearly what he'd done.

"I think it's extremely rude to speak in front of me in a foreign tongue," she observed, hoping to elicit at the very least an apology, at the most an explanation of what was said.

He shrugged. "I didn't want you to understand."

"This does concern me, you know."

"Not at all. As you've stated all along, it concerns your sister."

Julie felt her anger once again coming to the fore and Noah was saved from getting a berating of his own by the providential entry of the chief who wasn't looking exactly thrilled by the presence of Noah.

This time the two men spoke in Greek even though Julie knew they both spoke perfectly good English. She tapped her foot and stared out the window at a tree until Noah finally took her arm and led her out of the office.

"He could at least have apologized," she muttered as he hurried her out of the building.

"Greek police never apologize," he told her, leading her to a black Séat that had seen better days. "Anyway, he was only doing his job."

"Which was what?"

"Mossad asked them to pick you up and they were merely cooperating," he said, starting the engine and pulling off down the street. An air conditioner began to hum and Julie thought perhaps she'd live in his car during her visit rather than Emery's unair-conditioned apartment.

"You've been released in my custody," he informed her with a brief look in her direction.

"Nonsense."

"It's not nonsense at all."

"And I suppose that just happens to mean going dancing?"

"Got any better ideas?"

"Several. For starters, I'm supposed to meet Heracles back at the apartment at eight." She looked at her watch and saw that it was almost that time now. "And furthermore, if I'm not fed soon I might drop dead of starvation."

"The Hilton has some good restaurants—"

"Spare me your expertise on restaurants. What I'd like to hear is what was going on back there between the three of you."

"Kostas didn't know and Yotav wasn't telling."

"Wasn't *telling*? Is that all you've got to say?"

"I swear, Julie, I couldn't get a thing out of him. But don't worry, I'll get to my boss on this and he'll get to Yotav's boss and we ought to have this cleared up by morning."

"Which means that I know a hell of a lot more about it than you do, and you're supposed to be the professional spy."

"A much maligned occupation."

"With good reason!"

He gave his good-natured laugh and she was tempted to tell him what she and Heracles had figured out on their own. But she had a gut feeling that he was holding out on her, and in that case why should she be forthcoming? Still, she couldn't resist giving him a hint—just to tantalize him, keep him on edge. For some reason she had an urge to shake his even composure just as he seemed to shake hers.

"Keep it to yourself, then—it doesn't really matter. Heracles and I figured it all out and what Yotav said to me only confirmed it." Half truth, half lie, but it served her purpose. He didn't exactly drive off the road at the news, but his hands tightened on the wheel and the look of surprise he shot at her was gratifying. She pretended not to notice.

"So you are involved in something," he finally said.

"I'm not involved in anything except trying to find my sister."

"Perhaps I misjudged you."

"You didn't misjudge me at all except in your assumption that I was the type to take dancing!" And who was losing her composure now?

It didn't go unnoticed. "You sure remind me of Johnny."

"Then take my father dancing!"

Noah merely chuckled and she turned a stony look out the window of the car and watched in seething silence as they left Constitution Square and headed towards the Plaka. Why did she keep losing her temper with him? Julie asked herself, and answered immediately since it was an extremely easy question: Because she was attracted to him, that's why. She always found herself getting angry when she was attracted to a man, something a shrink no doubt would have much to say about. But perhaps it was just jet lag, being several hours behind where her body now sat, as was a good part of her brain. She couldn't really be interested in such a rumpled looking, bad-mannered man, could she?

Her body spoke a resounding yes, and she found herself crossing her arms over her chest and leaning in the direction of the door. She knew enough about body language to fake what she was feeling. A very strange turn of events since she had sexually gone to ground some time ago.

Julie gave him a glance out of the corner of her eye and saw that he was looking at her. She quickly averted her eyes but not before he said, "How about it, can I buy you some dinner?"

"I told you, I have to meet Heracles."

"That shouldn't take all night and you did say you were starving."

She gave an exasperated sigh. "*If* it doesn't take long with Heracles, and *if* you feel like waiting..."

He was double-parking in front of her building. What had before been a virtually deserted area was now filled with tourists taking up all the tables at the sidewalk cafés and milling in and out of the shops.

"I'll be across the street," he told her, "and if you're not back out in thirty minutes I'm eating without you."

She turned to him with a polite smile. "Thank you for getting me released, Colonel, and also for the ride home."

"How about for the offer of dinner?"

"I'll wait to thank you for that when I see if I get any." And it was beginning to look as though she never would, she thought as she climbed the stairs to Heracles's apartment. It was unlocked and empty, as was her own.

She went out on the balcony and saw that Noah had somehow acquired one of the sidewalk tables and seemed to be munching on something from a plate in front of him, a sight that infuriated her all out of proportion. But she was the one who was hungry, wasn't she? While he was the one who was eating.

She decided she could just as well await Heracles's arrival from a vantage point across the street, and only stopped to briefly use the bathroom in her hurry to get down there.

"That didn't take long," said Noah, looking up from a now empty plate.

"He wasn't there. What were you eating? Can I get some?"

"Did he leave a note?"

"No, I don't think he's been back yet. Would you order me whatever that was?"

He seemed in no hurry to do so. "They don't serve dinner here, just snacks."

"Well I've got to wait for Heracles, but I'll have several of those snacks."

"You'll spoil your dinner, Julie," he began, then saw her look and signaled for the waiter. "Would you like an ouzo to go with it?"

That really didn't sound like a good idea. "Is it possible to get beer here?"

"Of course," he said, giving an order to the waiter. A very good-looking waiter, Julie noticed, and then wondered about her noticing. How was it that entire months could go by in New York with her never giving any man a second look, and now suddenly they were all looking good to her? Not that an occasional student of hers didn't look appealing, but she always suppressed that temptation, leaving it to the male professors to seduce the students. But a regular New York man of an appropriate age? Forget it. If there were any around she sure hadn't noticed.

Julie forced her eyes away from the waiter and waited impatiently for her order to arrive, keeping an eye out for Heracles at the same time. Another attractive man—very attractive—but she'd always refused leftovers from her sister. Which reminded her that she was here to find her sister, not a man.

"A drachma for your thoughts?" Noah inquired.

"I was just thinking how good-looking Greek men are," she told him, thinking a little deflating of the ego would be good for him.

"They are, aren't they?" he agreed. "Even the old ones, they seem to get better and better with age. Unfortunately, the same can't be said for the women."

"You don't like Greek women?"

He shook his head. "The only disadvantage to my job, actually."

"A spy without women? That's a contradiction in terms."

"I never said I was without women."

She eyed him warily, wondering if this was a line of conversation she should pursue, then decided against

it. The women he used to see or saw now or might see in
the future were no more her business than the men in
her life were his. She could see he was waiting for some
kind of response, probably any kind of response just to
get one from her, but she passed it up and instead
looked around at the people occupying the other tables.

A great sea of tourists dressed in bright polyesters
seemed to have followed her from Greenwich Village, where they congregated in the summer months,
clear over the ocean to settle in the Plaka in Greece.
Only here, oddly enough, she'd have to consider
herself one of them. A patronizing pose, really, not
wanting to be mistaken for a tourist, and not even
such a smart pose when she thought about how very
easy it was to be a tourist. To be a tourist was to
escape accountability. Errors and humiliations don't
cling to you the way they do back home. You can just
drift across continents and through languages, sus-
pending for the moment the operation of sound
thought. You're allowed to be stupid; you are, in
fact, expected to be stupid. The entire mechanism of
the visiting country is geared to travelers acting
stupidly. You don't know how to talk to people, how
to get anywhere, what the money means, what time it
is, what to eat or even how to eat it. Acting stupidly is
the norm and you can exist on this level for weeks
without fear of dire consequences. Together with
thousands of other tourists you are granted im-
munities and broad freedoms. Tired, dysenteric,
thirsty, with nothing to think about but the next
event, you are allowed to just stagger about until it's
time to return home.

"I thought you were starving."

Her treatise on tourists evaporated at his words and she saw that the plate of snacks had been placed before her and she hadn't even noticed. She took a long drink of the cold beer, then started in on the olives and cheese and some kind of tiny fish that looked more like bait to her than anything meant for human consumption. It was food, though, and she ate it all.

"Now that the small talk and the food have been disposed of," Noah was saying, "I think it's time to get down to business. You hinted before that you knew something I didn't. I think it would be a good idea if you told me, Julie, so we can work together on this. I've noticed you have a slight tendency to view me as the enemy—"

"You must be used to that," she quipped.

"Not from American citizens, I'm not. Over here we're usually called on to help hapless citizens—"

"I can't imagine calling my local spy," she said, interrupting him once again.

"I'm not going to keep reiterating that I'm not a spy."

"Then why keep denying that you are?"

"Are you interested in hearing what my actual job is?"

"If you're interested in telling me."

He smiled with the barest hint of irritation. "I negotiate arms agreements for our government. I travel between here and Cyprus and Turkey, with a few stopovers in Washington. Rather mundane work if you discount the traveling."

Good cover story, she thought, and it might even be true. But that didn't answer the question of why an arms negotiator would be following a member of the Israeli secret police all over town.

"Tell me what you know, Julie."

It sounded like a formal request this time and she made the decision once again to trust him. If he wasn't what he seemed then she might be sorry, but at the moment she tended to trust him.

"It's not what I know, it's what we've surmised. My sister would have been at the airport at the time of the hijacking and we felt the two things must be connected."

His placid teddy-bear face seemed to rearrange itself into one of quick intelligence as she watched him grasp the meaning of what she'd said. "Yes, that would seem to add up."

"It was an El Al plane."

"I'm aware of that. And as yet no one's claimed responsibility for it. Yes, I think you've hit upon it."

Julie leaned back in her chair and crossed her arms. "Yes, I've done your work for you, now what are you going to do?"

"Have you told me everything?"

"No, but I've told you enough."

"Don't sabotage me at this point, Julie; not if you want your sister found. I have the facilities to investigate this—"

"So does Heracles."

"Who's where at the moment?"

She paused only briefly. "At the airport, hoping to talk to some of the witnesses."

He was nodding in agreement. "Good. Now tell me what you're holding back."

"Just what that Israeli said to me at the police station. He said he'd find it, that I had been observed."

"*It*?"

"That's what he said. And he didn't believe for a moment that I didn't know what he was talking about."

"Are you afraid your sister was taken hostage?"

The thought had not even occurred to her. Emery a hostage? It didn't seem possible. Her sister was just not the type. "No, that's not what I'm afraid of. Anyway, I didn't read anything about any hostages being taken. Do you know something I don't?"

"As far as we know none were taken. What was your sister doing out there? Returning home?"

Julie shook her head. "She was supposed to be filming an interview with someone arriving, but the interview never took place."

"Which would seem to lead to a logical conclusion. Your sister obviously filmed the hijacking in progress."

"And the Israelis want the film."

"Would your sister have been likely to suppress a film like that?"

"Not likely. The Emery I know doesn't feel *any* news should be suppressed."

"I think it more likely the Israelis want it suppressed. If they just wanted to see it they would have asked for our government's cooperation, but we haven't heard a word from them on it."

"Why would the Israelis want it suppressed? It was their plane, after all."

"That's what I'm going to have to find out." He was already getting up from the table and putting some money down to cover the bill.

Julie got to her feet. "Does this mean I don't get fed?"

He looked amused. "Stop by the office with me while I make a couple of calls and then we'll feed you, all right?"

"I'm supposed to be meeting Heracles."

"Who's obviously tied up somewhere. I'll get you back early."

And he would probably find out more with a few phone calls than Heracles would at the airport, she decided, following him to where he'd parked the car.

Bouzouki music could be heard from the outdoor gardens of tavernas as Noah maneuvered the car through the crowded, twisting streets. Once out of the Plaka area, he turned north on Sofia and sped down the tree-lined boulevard. On the way he pointed negligently to the Hilton, but what came to Julie's mind was eating, not dancing.

Not more than a mile further he pulled up in front of the American Embassy and parked the car. They went past a guardhouse with two armed Marines who waved them by, then they were inside the embassy where most of the office help had departed for the day and only a few people could be heard from behind the closed doors of offices.

Noah led her into the office, flipped on the light, then seated himself behind his desk and began to make his first call. Julie took a seat opposite him, noting the portrait of the President behind his desk and the American flag in one corner. On his desk, with its back facing her, was the kind of frame that generally housed a picture of the wife and kids and for the first time Julie wondered if Noah was married.

He could be, of course. It was her experience that married men came on just as strong as single men, and perhaps while his wife was back in Washington he availed himself of—well, of whatever was available. Meaning, at the moment, herself. Julie found she didn't like the thought.

Not that she didn't know plenty of women in New York who went out with married men. With three million more women than men in the city it was quite a temptation, but one she had so far resisted. And it wasn't because she was looking for a husband, either, because she wasn't; it was more that she didn't believe any man on earth deserved two women simultaneously. And here for the past hour she'd been wondering how soon she'd be able to go to bed with this man without making it too obvious that she wanted him. So much for fanciful, unproductive thinking!

He'd been making several phone calls in what sounded like several languages, and now he was going over the facts in English. With a show of impatience, Julie got out of her chair and began to wander around the office, ending up quite fortuitously behind his desk where she could get a look at what was in the silver picture frame.

A laughing young woman, her arms around two small children, a boy and a girl. The essence of a perfect family, she thought, glaring at the back of his head where his shaggy hair hung over his collar. The police chief was probably married, too. And Yotav. But not Heracles. But then she wasn't interested in Heracles.

Julie returned to her chair, crossing her legs and crossing her arms and deciding she'd prefer to eat alone after all. It was all for the best anyway; she had come over here to find Emery, not to end up in the arms of some questionable spy.

The questionable spy had now hung up the phone and was looking from her to the picture, a smug smile on his supercilious face. "Couldn't resist checking me out, could you?"

Involuntarily she felt her arms and legs tighten. "I don't know what you're talking about." Disinterested.

"We've been divorced ten years. This is an old picture, the kids are almost grown now."

She began to relax. "Your marital status is of no interest to me whatsoever."

"Like hell it isn't!"

"Colonel Majors—"

"And don't 'Colonel Majors' me, either. Relax. You're about to get that long-awaited dinner."

Why were men always telling her to relax as though tenseness were her major problem? She was quite relaxed. Extremely relaxed. And also extremely hungry. "I should call Heracles first and see if he got back."

"You have his number?"

Julie nodded, getting out her wallet and finding the slip of paper where her mother had written it down. Noah shoved the phone over towards her and she placed the call, but no one was answering at the other end. She hung up after twenty rings.

He took her arm as he led her out of the building and even a contact that casual made the hairs stand up along her arm. Her early-warning system was sending out signals and she wasn't sure how to interpret them. It was similar to the sensation she had on occasion when looking over the railing of a tall building—a terrible attraction to the idea of falling over. She went a long time between men and maybe it was time again.

His grip on her arm was tight with a tension that suggested sexual energy, inducing in her the telegraphic memory of sex, and in a nervousness unwarranted by his touch she pulled away from him once outside the building, electing to walk on her own. She heard him chuckle but didn't succumb to the temptation of asking him what was so funny.

"How about the Hilton?" he asked her.

"I didn't come to Greece to eat American food."

"There's a French restaurant—"

"Nor French."

"Greek, huh?"

"Greek." Firmly.

Once on Avenue Sofia again, he reached over and took her hand noncommittally, but this simple gesture felt like a low-voltage current was suffusing her left side. Noah kept his left hand on the steering wheel and with his right he was carelessly, casually rubbing her fingers, his attitude inattentive. She was trying to be as casual as he, trying to pretend there might be some other way to interpret the sexual signals that made the air crackle between them and caused her mouth to go dry. And then, of course, she could be wrong. What if she fell on the man like a dog on a bone only to discover that his meaning was merely friendly?

Julie felt mute, not uncomfortable, but languid. She found she couldn't think about anything because there was no sound between them, nothing said, not anything she could react to or fix on or with which to divert herself. He was, in fact, making it hard for her to breathe.

Noah released her hand as he parked in front of a building and she felt the tension ease as she got out of the car. They moved into the restaurant, their bodies close but his behavior polite, circumspect. He made no gesture towards her, verbally or otherwise, and she was suddenly disconcerted lest her sense of his pull was something generated in her and not reciprocated.

He glanced across the table at her when the waiter brought their menus. "Shall I order for us or would that offend your feminist sensibilities?"

"You're damn right it would," she told him, then glanced at her menu which was printed entirely in Greek. "On the other hand..."

He chuckled and set his menu aside. "I'll just ask for the specialty of the day. How about a bottle of wine?"

She nodded and looked around. No tourists, just very well-dressed, affluent-looking Greeks. She was looking as rumpled as Noah and felt they stood out from the crowd.

His leg brushed up against hers as he leaned across

the table to pour them wine. She took a sip and found it light-bodied and subtly aggressive, rather like she was feeling at the moment. It was mutual, it had to be, but if by chance it wasn't, she was determined to seduce him over dinner. She could feel the heat reach her face at the thought just before she heard his laugh. She slid a look up at him as her own laugh broke the spell and his eyes held hers only a little longer than they should.

"You're a puzzle to me, Julie."

"I'm a typical American—honest, open..."

"Devious, scheming..."

Caught in the act, she was flustered. "I'm no such thing!"

"I read one thing in your eyes and a split second later something else entirely is superimposed. I can't figure you."

His tone was ironic and the look he gave her was oddly sexual, full of a strange, compelling male heat. There was really nothing open or loose or free about him however candid he might seem, but she knew that it was precisely this trait that appealed to her. The teddy-bear exterior, the enigma beneath.

"I'm too old for games, Julie, are we going back to my place or not?"

"I thought you were here to help me. In an official capacity, of course."

He gave her a disappointed look. "Games again. I'll help you, Julie—I'll give you all the help I can. But I also very much want to make love to you and you're as aware of that fact as I am. I would also venture to guess you're feeling the same way, unless I've forgotten all I ever knew about women."

She was dragged out of the warm lethargy his words had induced in her by the arrival of their food. Julie now found she had lost her appetite and picked desultorily at the strange concoctions as she wondered whether she knew what she was getting into. She had about decided that not only did she know but she approved when out of nowhere she remembered she couldn't go to bed with him or anyone else. She might fancy herself a practical packer, but this time she'd been remiss.

She had a feeling he was taking her silence on the subject as assent, probably a maidenly, shy kind of assent that would have been foreign to her nature. Knowing that there was to be no sex in the offing, her appetite picked up and she not only finished off the three-course dinner but also insisted on dessert. He seemed impatient to leave, but humored her.

Back in the car again he once more took custody of her hand, but this time she thought she was under control. Since there was nothing concrete to anticipate, the excitement had lessened. But when he shifted in the seat slightly and pressed her hand between his legs, she felt a charge shoot through her and she groaned involuntarily. She heard his laugh, a low, excited sound, before he looked back at the road.

"We'll be there in a minute," he told her.

"Be where?"

"At my place."

"Please take me home, Noah." She hoped her voice conveyed the regret she was feeling but she really had no choice.

He pulled over to the side of the road and confronted her. "What kind of games are you playing now?"

"No games," she said, trying to make her voice matter-of-fact. "Listen, Noah, I just met you today, I could well be leaving tomorrow, and 'ships passing in the night' just isn't my style." Which sounded good, and she could see from his look of grudging respect that it had gone over fairly well, but the truth of the matter was that she had left her much-neglected diaphragm in New York and wasn't about to take back pregnancy with her as a souvenir of Greece. And she hardly knew him well enough to tell him the truth, although the temptation, she had to admit, was there. It had been a long time since she had met a man who appealed to her so much and she was sure that turning him down was more difficult for her than for him.

Noah pulled the car back on the road in a flurry of motion and she realized he wasn't taking it as well as she had thought. And she could hardly blame him. She'd been giving him signals all night and as soon as he followed through on them she'd shot him down. She knew she wouldn't take that kind of treatment very well herself. *Ships passing in the night?* Could she really have said something that corny? A woman almost thirty should have her act together better than that.

The Plaka was wall-to-wall people and he had to park some blocks from her apartment. They walked there in stony silence and when she got to the building she held out her hand to him, about to go into a speech thanking him for the dinner, etc.

He looked down at her for a long time before taking her fingertips and kissing them lightly, casually, looking at her the whole time. She felt like a switch was being turned on at the base of her spine as he turned her hand over and pressed his mouth into the palm. She didn't want him to do that, but she noticed she wasn't pulling her hand away. She watched him hypnotically, her senses dulled by the heat that was stirring way down, way deep, like a pile of rags beginning to smolder. All it needed was a spark, she was thinking as she felt her eyes close, mouth coming open against her will. At first there was too much hunger in the kiss, too much heat, but then like the welcome storm when the humidity's so high you think you can't bear it another minute, his kisses began to have a soothing effect, a lessening of the tension.

And with the lessening of tension came the thought, *Would it be worth the risk? Don't be foolish,* she told herself; *you're not a teenager who frequents abortion clinics. If you weren't adult enough to bring it, you're not adult enough to do it.*

As though sensing her thoughts were not on the kiss, he broke away from her and gave her a look that conveyed, "What next?"

"You'll let me know what you find out, won't you?" she asked in a shaky voice.

The look he gave her was of incredulity. "I've never been so wrong about a woman before."

"I'm sorry, Noah," she began, wondering whether she should level with him. He surely deserved it.

"You're like a typical tourist who comes on to the

Greek men and then yells 'rape' when the men take it seriously.'' He made a contemptuous gesture before turning around and heading back in the direction of the car.

Julie knew she deserved the harsh words, but that didn't make them any easier to take. She felt shaken as she mounted the stairs, pausing at Heracles's door to look inside and see if he was home yet. Nothing had changed since she'd been there earlier, so she headed up to Emery's apartment.

Stepping into the dark room, she was pushed up against the door by a warm body and then she heard someone say, "Turn on the lights."

Chapter Four

"Quiet!" she was ordered, but by that time the lights were on and she was given room to move so she didn't think screams were in order just yet. The three young people, two men and one woman, looked too much like her students to inspire fear, all of them dressed in the regulation jeans and T-shirts that made young people everywhere look the same.

At first she thought it must be the Israelis come to question her, but then she caught sight of Heracles leaning against the far wall and she relaxed. "You didn't need to attack me," she told him querulously.

"We couldn't be sure it was you," he told her, motioning the others to give her room. He introduced her to Halim and Samir, identifying them as Palestinians, and to Litsa, a Greek and daughter of one of his former comrades in the resistance.

"Palestinians?" Julie queried, but Heracles told her there wasn't time for explanations now, just to go into the bathroom with Litsa and do what she said.

"Now wait a minute," she began, but stopped at the look on Heracles's face. It was the kind of look her father had given her as a child whenever she tried to overstep the bounds of authority, which, being a good child, didn't happen too often.

"We're just going to dye your hair," Litsa told her, but if that was meant to be reassuring it struck out.

"I fail to see—"

"Look, Julie—we're taking you to your sister," said Heracles, "and we can't smuggle you out of here looking like that. With dark hair you'll be able to pass for a Greek." He walked over to where the shutters were closed and lifted one to peer out. "Two of Yotav's men are over there watching your building now, as is Colonel Majors."

"Oh, I don't think that's possible; he was furious with me when he left," she told him, joining him at the window to see for herself. Sure enough, there he was.

"Furious? What for, not cooperating with him?" asked Heracles.

"In a manner of speaking," mumbled Julie, glad he'd instantly jumped to the wrong conclusion.

"Hurry up, Julie, we have a plane to catch," said Heracles, and with some reluctance she followed the girl into the bathroom.

Heaven knows she wasn't crazy about her blond hair, but she'd never thought to dye it. Only after she was assured by Litsa that the dye was the kind that washed out did Julie lean her head over the sink and let the young woman administer the hair coloring. It was left to set for twenty minutes and only after it was rinsed out and partially towel-dried, her dryer still being in several pieces, did Julie take a look at herself in the mirror.

She was suddenly all of a piece: dark hair, dark eyebrows, dark eyes. For the first time she felt she fit together, looked the way she was meant to look. She fluffed up her hair with her fingers, watching the curls form, absolutely delighted with the change in her appearance. Now she looked like the Italian side of the family and she'd be able to go unnoticed in a crowd. She saw Litsa's reflection in the mirror grinning at her.

"You like?" the other woman asked her.

"I love it," Julie admitted.

"You look Greek now; no one will recognize you."

Julie took the towel and rubbed a corner of it in some soap, then scrubbed the traces of hair dye off her face. She wished she had some bright red lipstick to try with her new coloring, some vivid-colored clothing that she'd never felt she could wear before as a blonde.

"Are you finished in there yet?" Heracles was calling, and she stepped out of the bathroom to show him her new look.

He nodded his approval and asked Litsa to get out her passport. She handed it to him and he stood comparing the picture on it to Julie. "You'll do," he said, handing it to her.

She perused the face on the picture and thought it was close enough a resemblance to pass the inspection at customs. The only real difference was she was thinner than Litsa, but she could have lost weight since the passport was issued.

"Do you have any clothes with you those guys haven't seen yet?" Heracles asked her.

Julie went to the wardrobe and looked inside. Instead of her own, she pulled out worn Levi's and a khaki army issue shirt belonging to her sister and went into the bathroom to change. The shoes would have to stay the same, but practically everyone wore sandals similar to hers, and not too many men looked at a woman's feet the first thing. Or even the second.

She was still entranced by her change in appearance and couldn't keep her eyes off herself in the mirror. The hair dye seemed to have even changed the texture of her hair. It was still curly, but the curls were softer, not frizzing up anymore. Her formerly fine hair now had more body to it. She pushed out her lower lip defiantly the way Wally was wont to do and decided she now looked like a feminine version of her brother. Even her skin, which had always looked too dark for blond hair, now seemed to blend in to create a total look. Once in her sister's clothes she decided she could pass for any number of nationalities.

Julie left the building first with Samir, his arm around her and their heads bent close like lovers. She couldn't help darting a glance at Noah as they passed close to his table, but his eyes were elsewhere. She did note that he no longer looked angry, merely bored as he dragged on his cigarette and watched her building.

She gave Noah a surreptitious glance over her shoulder as Samir urged her on. Maybe they were ships passing in the night, but she had been very attracted to him and just to sneak away without another word to him bothered her. It was unfortunate that the first man she'd been attracted to in ages had to live several thousand miles away from her.

It was possible, of course, that she'd see him again. Despite where Heracles was taking her now, she'd have to return to Athens before going home in order to retrieve her clothes and her passport. On the other hand he might not care to see her since they hadn't exactly parted on the best of terms.

Samir hurried her around a corner and down two blocks, bumping into other pedestrians as they tried to gain speed, not stopping until they were some distance from the apartment and only then when he spotted a car and opened the door for her. Julie got in the backseat where Samir joined her.

"What now?" she asked him.

"Now we wait for the others." His answer was curt, his English tortured, so she sat in silence until Heracles and Halim arrived. Heracles got into the driver's seat and drove out of the Plaka before speaking.

"Are you all right back there, Julie?" he inquired.

"Fine, but I'd like to know where we're going."

"The airport, if we haven't been followed."

Julie looked out the back window but there were so many cars on the street she wouldn't have known whether one was following them. She said so, but Heracles told her not to worry, that he'd know.

"Where's my sister?"

Heracles looked at her in the rearview mirror. "It's better that you don't know until we're safely off the ground."

"She's in Greece, though, isn't she?"

"Wait, Julie—I will tell you as soon as the plane gets airborne, I promise."

Samir and Halim began talking in yet another language she didn't understand and under cover of their talk, she asked Heracles, "Why are Palestinians involved in this?"

"They live and work in Athens; they are friends."

It was an answer but not much of one. She was aware that Palestinians lived and worked in many countries, being displaced persons and all, but it seemed too coincidental that an El Al plane had been hijacked and now, for no discernible reason, she was riding in a car with two Palestinians. She was also sure the agent from Mossad would see something suspicious in that; she thought it suspicious herself.

Julie got out of the airport with her false ID with much more ease than she had got in with her real ID. Which said something for inept airport security, she supposed. She was, however, aware that countries didn't care who left, just who came in, and if they were leaving Greece, and she assumed that they were since they were taking off from the international airport rather than the domestic, the difficulty would come at the other end. They were flying on Olympic Airlines, but that didn't tell her much. As far as she knew, Olympic flew everywhere but to Albania, and if it had turned out Emery was indeed in Albania, she would have turned around and headed home and forgotten all about it anyway. Albania was not Julie's idea of a travel spot.

She sat with Heracles on the plane with Samir and

Halim two rows behind. As soon as the sign to remove their seatbelts flashed on, Julie turned to Heracles. "All right, where're we going?"

"Beirut." His tone was casual which didn't stop Julie from almost jumping out of her seat.

"You've got to be kidding!"

He smiled over at her. "You have never had an urge to visit Lebanon?"

"Not since their civil war, no."

"It's an interesting country—"

"It's a dangerous country! Furthermore, how are Samir and Halim going to get in? I was under the impression the PLO had been forced to leave."

"They're traveling with Greek passports, as are you."

"What's my sister doing getting mixed up with the PLO? Or did they actually hijack that El Al plane and involve her in some way?"

"Is that what you surmise?"

She didn't feel he was being as forthcoming as he had promised. "What I surmise is that she took a film of the hijacking, but I can't figure where the PLO comes in."

"Very good, you figured that out by yourself?"

"Don't be condescending with me, Heracles. Actually, Noah figured it out, but I was quickly arriving at the same conclusion."

"Noah? Who is this Noah?"

"Colonel Majors."

"You are now on a first-name basis with this man?"

"I'm an American, Heracles; we're just not that

formal." And she hadn't noticed Heracles insisting on last names. She'd been Julie to him from the moment they'd met. Of course there would be some difficulty, she supposed, in getting formal after meeting with a kiss. "You're not telling me why we're headed for Lebanon."

"I told you I was taking you to your sister." He was being evasive and she couldn't figure out why. She wasn't about to jump out of the plane simply because she didn't like his answers.

"What's Emery doing in Beirut?"

"Actually, she's outside of Beirut."

Julie was fast losing patience. "What's she doing outside of Beirut, then? Will you please tell me what's happening?"

He gave a large sigh as though he were being forced to contend with a nosy child and Julie gave her own sigh of exasperation in return. She had forgotten how foreign men tend to treat women like children. At least her. She doubted Emery ever had that problem, but then Emery never had any problems with men.

"Halim is a film student. He went out to the airport with your sister in order to learn from her and also to help her with her equipment. When the hijacking began, and it was all out in the open, your sister was all set up and ready to film, and so she got a record of it."

"But what's the point?" she asked, interrupting him.

"The point, my dear Julie, is that Halim recognized two of the hijackers as being from his village on the West Bank."

"So?" He just refused to give straight answers.

He smiled at her, his eyes lit up from within from the knowledge he had yet to impart. "So, they weren't Palestinians. They were Israelis."

He watched as the consequences of what he'd said sunk in. Israelis hijacking their own plane? To what purpose?

"Don't you see? They were Israelis dressed as members of the PLO."

"That doesn't make sense, Heracles."

"On the contrary, it makes perfect sense."

"Maybe to you," she muttered, trying to figure out why Israelis would dress up as Arabs to hijack their own plane. The more she thought about it the less sense it made, no doubt due in part to the fact that she'd by now been up too many hours and was getting punch drunk from lack of sleep.

"The PLO has been getting a lot of sympathy since Israel moved into Lebanon—from the press, from other countries. Further, they have been behaving themselves—no hijackings, no terrorist activities of any kind. This could have been a ploy on the part of the Israelis to gain some good publicity, unlike the adverse kind they have been receiving lately."

"I see. And Emery plans on exposing them?"

"That would appear to be the case."

Julie excused herself and climbed over Heracles's legs in order to visit the restroom. It was vacant, and she went inside and threw cold water on her face. Her eyes looked rather glazed from lack of sleep. They also looked frightened. Julie tried a smile to dispel the image, but the look of fear didn't recede. And why shouldn't she be afraid? She was headed for Beirut, for God's sake, one of the most dangerous places around at the moment. She'd be a fool not to be afraid. It was all very well for Emery to feel at home in the midst of danger, but that was Emery's choice. Her own choice was to be safely ensconced back in her New York apartment. Those who craved the excitement of danger were welcome to it; Julie only craved the quiet life.

When she got back to her seat Heracles was asleep and didn't even waken when she climbed over him to sit in the window seat. She thought of getting the flight attendant's attention and ordering a drink, but she was sure the distance from Greece to Lebanon was short and it wouldn't do to arrive half drunk when she'd need her wits about her to pose as a Greek. If they asked her questions she'd try to answer just yes or no, except that Greeks answered no by nodding their heads yes. Maybe she'd do better to just act stupid, let Heracles take care of it. He was the one who'd got her into this.

She was studying Heracles's sleeping face, thinking it was too appealing for any woman's good, when the flight attendant came by with glasses of carbonated lemon-flavored drinks that passed for lemonade in Greece. Julie took one, declined for Heracles, and wondered if her sister would welcome Heracles with open arms the way he'd welcomed her when he'd thought she was Emery. She had a feeling Emery wouldn't welcome *her* with open arms; she'd probably think her presence an intrusion. Maybe she should have refused to come. Her mother had said to find Emery; once she knew her whereabouts, didn't that constitute finding her? She didn't think Emery would be pleased having to share her adventure with her younger sister.

She woke up Heracles when the FASTEN SEAT-BELT sign came on. "By the way, Heracles, why are we going there? I'm sure Emery has things under control."

"She asked for you."

"Asked? What do you mean, did you talk to her?"

He nodded. "On the telephone."

"Why didn't you say so? What'd she say?"

"She said to bring you over, that she needed you. And do not ask me what for, because she did not say."

This was utter nonsense; Emery had never needed Julie for anything in her life.

As the plane banked to land, Julie saw a wide expanse of blue outside the window, water blending into sky. The sun had risen unnoticed by her as they flew. It was now morning in Beirut.

She had thought she was too tired to be nervous, but her legs felt weak as she stepped out on the landing field and, arm in arm with Heracles, headed for the low building. The flight had not been solidly booked: A few passengers looked like businessmen, the rest of the people in the airport terminal were military. She tried to concentrate on looking Greek, whatever that was. Halim and Samir stayed away from them; two Palestinians caught entering Beirut by the Israelis at this time would be in serious trouble. Julie still had faith that as an American she was somehow protected, until she remembered she was masquerading as a Greek.

To her relief, customs were minimal; the Lebanese seemed not to care who or what was entering their country at that time, at least not by way of the commercial airport. She yawned, and her hand automatically went up to cover her mouth as they headed out of the building. She caught sight of bullet-riddled taxis, armored vehicles, jeeps, and trucks and paused in disbelief at the sight. She had seen the war-torn country pictured countless times on the television news, in the papers, in news magazines, but none of it had prepared her for the reality in front of her.

She caught a glimpse of the sky where the sun still hung fairly low in the east in what seemed like an unmoving veil of smoke. Heracles hustled her into the backseat of a taxi where Halim and Samir were already seated. He got in front with the driver.

When she felt the hot wind against her face she realized the taxi had no windshield and dust whirling up by approaching convoys stung her face. The thick trunks of the palm trees on the green strip dividing the highway were minus their tops and she wondered if they'd been shot off. Just before turning into a traffic circle, the taxi stopped at a roadblock where they were checked by uniformed men. Samir whispered the word "Israelis" and she saw the young man was looking as fearful as she was feeling. She was afraid of the territory, though, not the Israelis. Despite Yotav, she didn't think of them as anything but friends. But then she saw a perforated machine-gun barrel pointing at her as she once again displayed her passport. She had thought she had known fear on occasion in New York when walking the streets alone at night, but it was nothing compared with what she was now feeling. She had a sudden urge to go to the toilet and tried to control it.

The sea was beside them as the driver drove off down a broad coastal avenue, and through the rear window it appeared innocent and out of place. The driver turned off on a side street by the Cape of Beirut and she saw the Hotel Commodore, a newish-looking building surrounded by other commercial and residential buildings interspersed with a few still-standing smaller ones. To the west, over towards the point of the Cape, was a lighthouse, and below it a little mosque, its minaret equipped with loudspeakers pointing in all directions.

She swallowed, trying to ease the dryness in her throat. "What are we doing at a hotel?" she asked Heracles as they got out of the taxi and she clung to his arm.

"We'll eat, rest awhile, then try to find a car for hire. Anyway, it's the safest place to be at the moment."

The sides of the hotel had gaping holes and most of the window glass had been blown out. It didn't look safe to Julie, but it did look preferable to standing around under the relentless sun. She had thought Athens hot, but Beirut made Athens feel air-conditioned.

She wondered, not for the first time, what she was doing there. Beirut? She must be crazy. Surely her mother hadn't meant for her to rush into one of the most dangerous spots in the world. And yet if Emery were there... But Emery was always running head-long into danger, she thrived on it. Conversely, Julie thrived on the normal, the mundane; she even eschewed Washington Square Park the majority of the time. This city might have airlines still servicing it, hotels and restaurants might still be in business, but it was, purely and simply, a war zone, and she couldn't remember volunteering for action.

"Stop the war, I want to go home" she felt like shouting to the rooftops, but she didn't, and knowing Beirut, the rooftops were probably manned. Julie was trying to summon up the words to tell Heracles that she wanted out, but her vocal chords didn't appear to be functioning. Her stomach was functioning, however; it was turning over at an alarming rate.

"Are you all right?" Heracles was bending down to her, looking concerned, but his casual attitude was more suited to the Plaka than to Beirut.

"I've just never been to war before," she finally managed to say, her hand clutching her stomach as he led her into the lobby of the hotel.

"You'll get used to it." She was sure by his words that he meant to reassure her. But what was reassuring about being told she's get used to it? She didn't want to get used to it. She wanted to get out of there before she was forced to get used to it.

"I think this was a bad idea, Heracles. I think what we ought to do is turn right around and go back to Athens."

"Emery is depending on you."

Emery had never in her life depended on Julie so

why start now? If this was Emery's idea of a vacation spot, fine. She could have it. Julie had always found Miami horrendous, but it was far preferable to this.

Even as she was voicing her protests, Heracles was registering them in the hotel. A bellboy, his oily hair flattened as if permanently, escorted them to the elevator. It occurred to Julie that the elevator might be a risky place if shells were to hit the building and she found herself holding her breath until they were out of the enclosure and walking down a long hallway.

She stood looking at the room. It looked so normal, so like any hotel room anywhere, that she was nonplussed. "Come," Heracles was saying to her, "let's get something to eat."

Julie was eyeing the bed. "Couldn't we rest for a while first?"

"No time."

"Then why did we get rooms?"

"In case we're checked up on. Come, we are to meet the others in the dining room. You'll feel better with some food in your stomach."

She gave him a disbelieving look before following him out of the room. Food wouldn't help her stomach; a nice safe place was what her stomach needed.

Samir and Halim were already at a table and they offered her a glass of arrack, a clear, vicious aniseed liquor that they suggested she dilute with water. She didn't take them up on their suggestion. She drank it down straight and didn't care that her insides ended up feeling raw. And found that, strangely enough, her stomach felt better for it.

They were served a fish mezze consisting of grilled and boiled fish and a variety of salads and vegetables served in small dishes with a few strips of unleavened bread. She picked at her food until Heracles told her it might be her last meal for a while and she should finish it. Julie hoped it was her last meal for a while: Every bite was detestable.

While they sat drinking thick, unpalatable coffee, Samir left the table, returning in a few minutes to say that he'd found a car for hire, a driver who'd agreed to take them to Tripoli. Julie was about to ask where Tripoli was when she saw the men entering the hotel dining room. She was the only one facing them and she quickly averted her eyes, saying softly to Heracles, "Yotav and two men just came in."

He didn't react visibly. "Have they seen you?"

"I don't know, but he wouldn't recognize me with dark hair, would he?"

"Perhaps not, but he will recognize me. What's he doing now?"

Julie looked towards the door. "Just standing there, looking around."

Heracles seemed to be taking his time thinking over the situation and as the seconds passed Julie began to tremble. Then she saw Yotav begin to move in their direction, somewhat impeded by a waiter balancing a tray just in front of him. "He's coming," she said to Heracles, and when he still sat there she said, "Listen, I'll turn left when I get out of the hotel and just keep going. Pick me up if you can." Without waiting for any confirmation, Julie launched herself out of her chair and plunged directly into the path of the oncoming waiter. There was confusion as several drinks flew off the tray, the contents spraying over Yotav and his friends as the sound of breaking glass brought a monetary lull in noise to the dining room. Head down, Julie kept going, not even looking back to see what Heracles was doing.

She was halfway across the lobby when she saw Noah by the registration desk, deep in conversation with the man behind the counter. It didn't even occur to her to run to him and ask for his protection; she was committed to helping her sister now and she was certain he'd try to stop her.

The sunlight was blinding when she got outside. She turned left and headed up the sidewalk, instinctively staying as far away as possible from the plate glass windows in the buildings. She noticed that the people around were scurrying, taking the shortest routes, maneuvering on the streets through lines of honking, thrusting cars. No one glanced at her as she hurried on. The air was fetid and palpably sticky and she looked with envy at the loosely billowing garments worn by the women. Her own clothes were clinging wetly to her body and seemed to be shrinking in size.

Two blocks away from the hotel she stopped and pretended to be admiring the wares of a sidewalk vendor. She didn't know what the man was saying to her, so she kept shaking her head and watching out of the corner of her eye for Heracles and the others.

An ancient Mercedes slowed down and she was about to make a run for it when Heracles jumped out of the passenger seat and motioned her inside. She saw the door wouldn't latch, but that seemed a minor consideration at the moment. Heracles was getting in the driver's side and forcing the driver over next to Julie where his corpulent body pressed up against hers, raising the temperature in the car to an unbearable level.

Heracles drove with one arm out the window, totally relaxed. He could have been going for a Sunday afternoon drive in the country. "That was quick thinking," he said to her. "Our Israeli friends were still mopping themselves off when we made our escape."

She didn't think it had been quick thinking, more like momentary panic. "Did you see Colonel Majors in the lobby?" she asked him.

"So, they are all here, are they?"

Obviously he hadn't seen him. For someone who had been in the resistance he didn't appear to be too observant. His eyes seemed to be more often on the rearview mirror than on the road and she tried to twist around in the close quarters and see out the back. "Are we being followed?" she finally asked.

"I can't tell," he said, "but if we are, it won't be for long. We're approaching PLO territory and I doubt that the Mossad will want to venture in there."

They were headed for Tripoli, driving for over an hour along the coast. Heracles cut the curves, passed everything. Julie slumped against the upholstery while the car radio blasted out Middle Eastern laments that went on and on, never ending. The back of Julie's head began to pound.

At Chekka they turned off into the mountains and

she could see their yellow dust clouds in the switch-backs below. They drove through villages where sheep and dozing dogs lay in the shadows; at the door of a hut, young civilian guards merely raised their heads for a moment and left their rifles lying across their knees. Heracles swung the car around as the music cascaded out of the side windows. In a curve they caught sight of the sea again, far below, a single glittering, dazzling reflection. Julie held her face to the wind and concentrated on breathing.

There was a lovely view of Beirut, laying under a thin, transparent layer of haze; in the south, Samir pointed out where tires were being burned, causing the sky in that direction to turn a dirty gray. The smoke was billowing up from a few points close to-gether, climbing tenaciously and spreading slowly up the mountain terraces. Suddenly, as they rounded a bend, they saw some rocks lying on the road, with clods of sticky, slatey soil and a few uprooted young trees and shrubs strewn about. Heracles drove at full speed to within a few yards, then stepped hard on the brake and reversed as fast as he could into the curve, where he stopped. Not a soul was in sight.

The men got out of the car as they reached the debris and cleared a passage. Julie watched them in silence, feeling numb. They went on, and shortly before Ba'abda they passed through a number of checkpoints where they were simply waved on as they drove up to the guards at a crawl. The soldiers were mostly young with round, friendly faces. At the checkpoint just outside Ba'abda they were told they couldn't drive on toward 'Aley-h, and then, looking to where a guard was pointing, they saw over to the southwest metallic reflections just below a ridge, thin gun flashes and little puffs of smoke.

"We have to go the rest of the way by foot," Heracles said matter-of-factly.

"How far?" she asked.

He put a sweaty arm around her shoulders. "You are doing fine; it won't be much farther. A nice stroll to work off our lunch."

Julie was feeling too hot and tired to even think. She stumbled along the rock-strewn path behind Heracles, her eyes squinting against the sun. Soon they reached the course of the Nahr el Damour where they also caught up with a patrol who motioned for them to follow. The water was clear, sending up a rosy spray over a steep cascade. At the top of the sheer cliff on the other bank was a mortar emplacement with four men sitting on the parapet dangling their legs and waving to them. They had to pick their way carefully across the stream on rocks placed so that it was easy to cross dryshod. Farther downstream they could see the stumps of the pillars that had once supported the blown-up sandstone bridge. There, too, they could see, on the other side, the gravel road that had connected Deir el Qamar and Damour before the bridge was destroyed. It wound its way from the ruined bridge downstream, as if there had been no interruption.

By this time they were only a few hundred yards from the coast road. The sea shimmered, soft and enticing through the arches of the viaduct. They found themselves following some soldiers, who were leaving the watercourse and scrambling up the bank. At the top they sank down onto pine needles and mossy rocks; ammunition cases were standing around everywhere. There was a machine-gun emplacement in a copse of pines.

What they could see of the town from here was a collection of huddled yellow houses pushed up the slope, from this distance an orderly scene, but from close up the edges and contours, the walls and corners, seemed as if crumbled by an earthquake, so that seen from even closer everything shifted into unfocused outlines.

Two armed men who had followed them came up and asked whether they were ready to go on. They got up and walked off with the men. Down in the town they hurried through the gardens, crouching as they ran, although at that moment no shots were being fired. At the end of a long alley, completely deserted and desolate-looking, she could see the busy traffic in the center of town. The little square, an intersection, seemed to catch all the sunlight, like a stage. Trucks and jeeps were blocking the alleys. Furniture and household goods—bales of material, crates, rugs—were being carried out of burning buildings. They were escorted to a small flat-roofed building, more of an army hut.

She had safely maneuvered rocks and streams only to trip, at the last minute, over the wood threshold of the hut. She landed on her twisted ankle, an involuntary cry of pain escaping her.

"Stupid klutz," Julie muttered to herself, moving

her ankle out from under herself and feeling it to see if it was broken.

Appearing as if from nowhere out of the shadowy darkness, a figure suddenly materialized in front of her. At first Julie thought it was a man. Her eyes traveled upwards from the combat boots, past the army fatigues, then came to rest on her sister's face.

"Welcome to Lebanon." Emery, looking sexy despite the male clothing she wore, grinned down at her.

Chapter Five

Her sister the terrorist, Julie thought to herself as she eyed Emery's getup, complete right down to the combat boots. She had noticed in the past that her sister seemed to take on the coloration of whatever group she was involved with at the moment.

With a slight show of reluctance, Emery reached down and offered Julie her hand, pulling her none too gently to her feet. Julie found her ankle was sore, but not too sore to stand on, although already she could see it was starting to swell. In her relief to see Emery safe, she reached out to give her a hug, but Emery held her off in her usual way, then quickly kissed both her cheeks, European style, which wasn't her usual way at all.

Heracles got the same treatment when he tried to take Emery in his arms, Julie noted with amusement. If there had been something between them before, it now seemed to be off.

"Why Lebanon, Emery?" she asked her sister, wanting to hear a good reason why she herself had been summoned to the place.

"What I'd like to know is what you were doing in Athens."

Julie glanced over at Heracles. "Ask him—he's the one who called Mother."

This was clearly news to Emery. She turned a scathing look on Heracles. "Please explain yourself," she demanded.

Heracles looked somewhat cowed. "I got worried about you when you didn't return."

"So you called my *mother*?"

Heracles shrugged. "I thought she should be informed."

Arms crossed, Emery began to stride back and forth. "Tell me something, Heracles; if I had been a man, would you have called my mother?"

"Emery, I apologize; I misjudged the situation."

"I think it was me you misjudged." She turned to Julie. "And Mother sent you running over here to rescue me? Is that it?" Her voice was filled with scorn.

"Just to find you, that's all. There was no mention of rescuing." Emery had always had the ability to make Julie feel inept and that hadn't changed.

"Ridiculous," murmured Emery.

Julie had about had it with Emery's condescending manner. It occurred to her that Emery treated her very much as men treated her, as someone not to be reckoned with. "Ridiculous? Is that all you can say? I wasn't eager to drop everything and go looking for you, you know. Nor was it my idea to dye my hair and hotfoot it to this godforsaken place. As far as I'm concerned, Emery, you can just—"

"The hair color suits you," Emery interrupted her. A pause, then, "Thank you."

"Anyway, now that you're here I can use your help."

"You still haven't answered my question," Julie persisted. "Why Lebanon?"

"It seemed a good idea at the time. Safe harbor and all that. And I've got some marvelous footage while here. Did Heracles tell you about the filmed hijacking?"

Julie nodded.

"It's going to cause a sensation when it's shown, quite make my reputation."

Julie had thought the hut empty, but now several dark forms detached themselves from the shadows, materializing by Emery's side. One put his arm around her in a proprietary manner and Julie could have sworn she saw her sister lean into him. A short exchange was conducted in a foreign tongue, and then Emery said, "Julie, this is Mohammed."

Julie almost laughed aloud at the name, which struck her as a cliché. New York was filled these days with Mohammeds, most of whom stood around in robes on Sixth Avenue selling incense.

She nodded to the man dressed identically to Emery in fatigues. Another looker, of course; the only kind Emery seemed to attract. Then Emery introduced Mohammed to Heracles, and Julie sensed the tenseness in them as they shook hands, looking for a moment as though each was trying to wrestle the other to the floor.

The big surprise was the others. So this was what the PLO looked like, she mused. She had expected bogeymen, and instead they looked younger than her students. Not even the Kalashnikov assault rifles they carried slung over their shoulders could dispel the feeling in her that she was among a group of children playing at war. But she knew this kind of thinking was spurious; they were indeed involved in war, she'd seen ample evidence of that fact everywhere in Lebanon.

"I need to get the film to New York," Emery told her in the kind of casual manner that belied the fact that the film was anything but the usual tourist fare.

Julie, whose ankle was beginning to ache, looked around for something on which to sit. She finally spotted a wooden case and used it for a chair. She pushed up her left pant leg and saw the rapid swelling. "Do you have any ice?"

"I'm afraid not," Emery told her. "We're lucky to have water."

"I think you should know, Emery, that Mossad agents as well as Colonel Majors of the CIA have followed us here."

"Impossible. They wouldn't dare come here."

"Well, maybe not exactly here, but they were in Beirut when we left."

"Heracles said you'd been mistaken for me."

"I think Mossad still thinks I am, but Colonel Majors knows the story."

"I had thought of using you for a diversion while I fly to the States," said her sister.

Julie shook her head. "Afraid not, Emery. I didn't want to come here in the first place; if anyone's leaving, it's going to be me."

Emery looked disconcerted at finding her sister

with a mind of her own. "I don't think I should let it out of my hands."

"You're just going to have to trust me, Emery. I'll try to get it out for you, but I'm not staying around here any longer."

"How are you going to get out? They'll search your bags, Julie."

"Yes, but they won't search my ankle." Julie grinned.

"Your ankle?"

Julie nodded. "You have any bandages around here?"

"Yes, I suppose so."

"What we'll do, Emery, is wrap the bandage around my ankle, with the film in between the layers. Unless, of course," she hesitated, "doing so would expose the film."

Emery was looking at her with something like awe. "No, it's been processed. Julie, that's a fantastic idea! Who ever would have thought it of you?"

Julie basked for a moment in her sister's rare praise, albeit somewhat tempered. "Do you think it'll work?"

"It's better than any idea I've come up with. In that case I'll be the one to create the diversion. I'll go to Beirut first, show myself where Mossad can see me, and meanwhile you'll be leaving the country."

"Your sister's quite inventive," Heracles said to Emery. "She was the one who got us out of Beirut."

Emery didn't seem eager to hear Julie praised still further. "You'll have to tell me all about it later. For now, we have some work to do."

It was evening when Julie returned with Heracles, but already the city was closing up. Only a few cars raced along the Hamra, private cars painted in green and yellow camouflage. The steel shutters of the stores, garages and entrances had been lowered, the chairs in front of the cafés piled up and chained together. She saw a rat cross the street, as straight and unfaltering as a toy animal being pulled along on a string. Armed men patrolled the streets wearing odd bits of uniform, as well as blue jeans and padded parkas. Occasionally the better-dressed Israeli soldiers were to be seen.

They couldn't get a flight out until late that night and Julie asked if she might use the room they'd paid for at the hotel in order to get some sleep.

"Better not," said Heracles. "We're assuming your sister's been picked up already, but we can't be certain. We don't want to confuse the issue by having both of you there at the same time. We'll get some food; that should pick you up."

She thought twelve hours of sleep were more likely to pick her up, but didn't argue. Julie felt nervous about the thickly wrapped ankle, aware all the time that it wasn't just bandages. The more she tried to put the knowledge of the film out of her mind, the more she seemed to dwell on it.

Few people were on the streets of Beirut. Now and then flickering, fiery reflections lit up the darkening sky, followed by a series of detonations of varying strengths. It reminded her of electrical storms in New York. They turned into a side street and walked down the steps to the Bar des Lilas, its doorway outlined by a string of Christmas tree lights.

As Julie's eyes adjusted to the dim interior she saw the scantily clad women sitting in a row at the bar, smiling. Their smiles dimmed when they saw that she was with Heracles and she felt some unjustified guilt at depriving them of a customer. Heracles led her past the bar to the red velvet upholstered booths in the back where he waited while she slid in first, then sat by her so that his back was to the wall and they were both facing the door.

She ate what was offered, drank some arrack diluted with water, and waited until it was time to leave for the airport. She was beyond being tired, she felt almost in a coma, unaware of everything but her desire to be back home in New York. Heracles had to help her out of the bar when it was time to leave.

Just the two of them flew back. She didn't see Halim and Samir on the flight and didn't inquire as to their whereabouts. She was too tired to even worry about Greek Customs and gave little thought to what was wrapped around her ankle. Not that she thought it illegal: drugs were illegal, not film. They were waved through customs with no difficulty. While they were at the airport Heracles made her a reservation on the morning flight to New York and now all she cared about was getting back to Emery's apartment and obtaining a few hours' sleep.

They got a taxi to the Plaka where tourists were still milling around, the tavernas filled with the sound of shirt-sleeved Athenians singing. The Acropolis continually sprang into glaring relief and disappeared in the course of one of the *son et lumière* spectacles that were currently turning all the wonders of the world into something more appropriate for the Times Square area, in Julie's opinion. Still, Athens was sanity itself compared to Beirut and she was thankful that she'd come out of the trip unscathed except for a slightly swollen ankle.

Heracles let her off in front of the building and retained the taxi. ''I'll stop by your place in the morning to take you to the airport,'' he said to her out the window of the cab.

''Don't bother,'' she answered, but the taxi had already pulled off. Just as well, she doubted she'd wake up in time by herself and she'd pack before going to bed so that she could be ready five minutes after he arrived.

She opened the door to her sister's apartment and turned on the light. Standing by the shuttered doors was Noah in the same clothes he'd been wearing in the lobby of the hotel in Beirut.

His eyes narrowed only slightly at the sight of her changed appearance, and then he was asking, ''Where've you been?'' His look was searching, his tone preemptory.

She sagged against the door, her mind too tired to function properly. She thought she was glad to see him; then again, she was even happier to see a bed.

''Who was the man in the taxi with you?''

She ignored him, going over to the bed and sitting on the edge to remove her sandals. She made sure he caught sight of the bandages as she did so.

''What happened to your ankle?''

An ignition seemed to be turned on in her mind and it slowly began to function again. This wasn't the

Noah whom she'd desired; this was a visit from the CIA. "I turned it—climbing up to see the Acropolis." She was prepared for his concern, ready to tell him it was properly bandaged and really not serious at all, but he still stood by the window, studying her, and didn't pursue the matter of her ankle.

"The hair. Is that a wig?"

She'd forgot her change in appearance. How had he so readily recognized her, or was it that he had assumed it was she entering the apartment? "I had it dyed."

"For any particular reason?"

She propped up the pillows against the wall and leaned back on the bed. Why was she being questioned when she was too tired to think? "I just felt like a change. No, that's not quite true. What I really wanted was not to stand out in the crowd. Do you like it?"

"You took time out from looking for your sister to get your hair done?" He sounded disbelieving.

Her mind switched into overdrive. "All right, so I had an ulterior motive. I figured with dark hair I'd be able to avoid Yotav. And I was right: I haven't seen him since I had it done. Anyway, I like the change; I may even keep it this way." Her hand went up to finger the dark curls. She had to act normal, be believable; she wasn't out of the country yet.

Noah dragged a wooden chair up to the bed and straddled it, his arms folded on top of the back, facing her. There was a dangerous look to his eyes she hadn't seen before. He took his time, reaching into a pocket and bringing out cigarettes, then lighting one, not even looking around for an ashtray but flicking the used match onto the floor. A cloud of smoke was billowing around his head before he spoke. "Where have you been all day?"

"I really don't think that's any of your business."

"If you want me to be honest with you, Julie, start being honest with me."

She sighed. "Heracles said I'd just be in the way, so while he was trying to find Emery, I played the tourist."

"It looks as though 'playing the tourist' wore you out."

She managed a smile. "It is wearing, isn't it? I'm exhausted, Noah, couldn't this wait until morning?"

"Aren't you even going to ask me what I've found out?" He was leaning close to her, watching her eyes.

Julie closed her eyes and rolled onto her side. "All right, tell me what you've found out."

"What's the matter with you, Julie? You don't even sound interested."

"Of course I'm interested; it's just that I'm so tired. Anyway, I'm beginning to get annoyed with Emery." She noticed his frown. "Well, not exactly annoyed, but I don't see that I'm doing any good being over here. If Emery's got herself into a mess, she can just get herself out. I'm an economist, not a private detective." She tried to make her voice sound petulant, and from his disapproving look felt she'd succeeded.

"If you're interested, I've found out some information." He waited for a reaction from her and got none. "You're no longer interested in your sister?"

"Of course I'm interested, just tell me."

He got up from the chair and walked out on the balcony, taking one last drag from his cigarette before throwing it over the side of the railing. Coming back into the room he ignored the chair and stood leaning against the shutters. "This is confidential, Julie. May I assume you'll treat it as such?"

"Are you swearing me to secrecy?"

"Something like that."

"Can I tell my family?"

He nodded. "This has turned into somewhat of a delicate situation. It seems that your sister filmed what has subsequently turned out to be a phony hijacking."

"How can it be phony? I read about it in the papers."

"Phony in the sense that the hijackers weren't Arabs; they were Israelis." He was watching closely for her reaction and she managed to widen her eyes appropriately.

"Why would Israelis hijack their own plane?"

He expelled the breath he'd been holding. "It seems a fanatic religious group who'd been told to leave their homes on the West Bank took matters into their own hands. They thought if they made it look as though the PLO were into hijacking again, the government would rescind the order and they could remain."

"Then the government wasn't involved?"

"On the contrary, they're finding it highly embarrassing; hence their efforts to retrieve the film."

She folded her arms across her chest. "And our government is helping them."

"Julie, it's in our interests too not to have Israel embarrassed at this time. Negotiations are going on right now over Lebanon—"

"And the truth matters not at all!"

"I hadn't thought you were political."

"I'm not political, but I don't see any justice in having this hushed up. Why should the Arabs be indirectly blamed for something they didn't do?"

"It's blown over in the press already."

"That doesn't make it right, Noah."

"All of this is past history anyway. The Mossad picked up your sister a couple of hours ago. In Beirut."

"She was in Beirut?" All innocent surprise.

"Yeah. She doesn't have a hell of a lot of sense is all I can say."

"Is she all right?"

"As far as I know. A representative of our government is with her, so you needn't worry. All she'll have to do is turn over the film—"

"And if she won't?"

"I believe she's already agreed."

Julie hoped she'd be able to get out of the country before they found out Emery didn't have the film. She was sure her sister would lead them a dance, though, giving Julie enough time to get back to New York. "Well, that's that, then. I guess I can go back home."

"Couldn't you stay in Athens for a few days? See the sights?"

"I saw them today. No, I'd really prefer to leave. I hate all this intrigue, Noah; I just want to go home and get back to normal."

"Does that mean going back to being blond?"

She managed a smile. "I haven't decided about that just yet."

He was walking toward the bed, unbuttoning his shirt and loosening the belt at his waist at the same time. Her mind shifted into high gear. "What do you think you're doing?"

"I'm spending the night with you, making sure you get to the airport without any hassle."

"Noah, I'm perfectly capable of taking care of myself."

"I want to, Julie." He was moving her legs up on the bed, being careful of her bandaged ankle.

"Noah, I'm not going to—"

"Yea, I know; ships passing in the night. I just want to be close to you, hold you." He was beside her on the bed, clad only in his T-shirt and briefs, and she wasn't too tired to notice that what she'd taken for flab when he'd been dressed, was mostly hard muscle. Well, there was a little extra weight around the waist. Just enough to make her feel comfortable about undoing the button of the tight jeans at her own waist that had been impairing her breathing.

Face to face on the bed, he put his arms around her and drew her close. She could smell the saltiness of his skin. She fit her head to the curve of his shoulder and the last thing she remembered was his lips pressing against her hair.

She awakened to see him propped up on one elbow, gazing down at her. She blinked, remembered the previous night's events, and glanced at her watch.

She had about an hour before Heracles should be coming by to get her. She started to get up but he pinned her back down by placing one firm hand against her shoulder.

"I need to get up, Noah."

He didn't answer, just bent down so that the sunlight was blocked. She didn't see his lips until they were pressed against hers and then something inside of her responded to the touch and she found her arms circling his back as her mouth relaxed and slowly opened. Peripherally she was aware of noises in the street, of doors being slammed, of women calling out in Greek, but her attention was focussed on what was happening much closer as his tongue entered her mouth and took territorial possession.

She couldn't have had more than three hours sleep and the kissing took on a dreamlike quality. His lips seemed to be in slow motion, as were his hands, moving up and down her back and she was finding it so restful, so relaxing, so lulling, and very, very sensual. She lazily probed her own tongue around the wet terrain of his mouth as she adjusted her body more comfortably against his. She closed her eyes and found herself wishing she could remain like this all day, take each step in the steady progression of lovemaking and the devil take the risk. It would be so easy just to give in, take a chance, live dangerously for once in her life.

His hands moved further down her back, still further until they were curving her derriere and pressing her close to him, so close she could feel his erection and she found herself trembling at the touch. Her hiatus from sex had made her forget the deep pleasure inherent in being so close to a man and she made a small sound of pleasure that he misinterpreted as a go-ahead as she felt one of his hands reaching for the zipper on her jeans. She shouldn't have allowed it to progress so far; now, once again, she would be put in the position of being thought a tease, and justifiably so.

She reached down to trap his hand with her own and watched as his eyes opened warily. "No, Noah; I'm sorry. . ."

His hand refused to move. "You want me as much as I want you."

"What I want and what I'm prepared to do are not the same things."

He rolled over onto his back and flung one arm across his eyes. "What do you require, Julie, a declaration of love first? I thought things had changed, that two people who liked each other could now enjoy each other without all that added baggage."

And speaking of added baggage, she realized his leg was on top of her bandaged ankle and she hadn't even felt it. She now sat up and reached down to extricate it, making enough of a production of it that she saw him remove his arm and look down the length of the bed at her.

"I'm sorry—I forgot about your ankle. Did I hurt it?"

"It's all right, I think."

"You want me to take a look at it?"

"No, honestly—it's okay. A little sore but I'll see a doctor when I get home if it's still bothering me."

"You know I like you a hell of a lot, Julie."

She turned to look at him. "I like you, too, it's just that..."

"You're not a virgin, are you?"

She managed a laugh. "No, I'm not a virgin."

He swung his legs over the side of the bed and lowered his face in his hands. "Then it must be me."

She had a sudden urge to explain the circumstances to him, but decided it wouldn't alter anything if she did. She only had about thirty minutes now to get rid of him and be ready to leave for the airport when Heracles arrived. And she also knew herself well enough to know that, feeling about him as she already did, it would only take sex to propel her feelings of like for him into love, and there was no point in falling in love with a man who after today she'd never see again. They quite literally lived in two different worlds and it was just pure bad luck that it couldn't have happened with someone closer to home.

He was looking disappointed and somewhat desolate, exactly the way she was feeling herself. She longed to put her arms around him and tell him that for some unaccountable reason he was already very dear to her, but she had a feeling that wasn't what he wanted to hear. She knew from experience about the fragility of the male ego and understood that what he wouldn't want to hear was that she liked him and wanted him but it just wasn't to be. And while at this point she might feel free enough with him to confess the absence of her diaphragm, there was no longer enough time to remedy the situation, and she couldn't explain the lack of time to him. She'd just have to get rid of him quickly if she cared at all about getting Emery's film back to the States, and getting rid of him quickly probably meant getting him angry with her once again.

Julie sighed. She was not at all used to treating men so shabbily, particularly a man she liked so much. "You're just. . .just really not my type, Noah. I like you, but. . ." She left the sentence hanging as she waited for his reaction.

It was immediate. He got to his feet and retrieved his clothes from the floor, not even glancing at her again as he quickly dressed. "As a matter of fact, you're not my type, either," he said as he paused by the door. "I generally like honest women. It doesn't even matter what they look like as long as they're straight with me. Well, Julie—it's been a pleasure, as they say. Only in this case. . ." He was out the door before she could answer and it slammed in his wake, then she waited as the sound of his footsteps receded.

And that is that, she thought to herself as she headed for the bathroom for a wash-up, a shower being out of the question with the film around her ankle. *Scratch one good man and just hope you don't regret it when you're back in New York where good men are scarce, if not totally nonexistent.*

"I wasn't worried a bit with you in charge," her mother had said to her when she'd called from the airport in Athens before boarding the plane. Not that she'd told her mother much, leaving Lebanon out entirely. She merely said that she'd found Emery and everything was now under control.

The United States Customs' agent gave her a hard time at JFK, but not over anything important. He seemed to consider it frivolous that she'd gone so far and spent so much for such a short trip, and he persisted until she pulled up her pant leg and showed him her bandaged ankle, feeling a heady sense of danger as she flaunted the contraband brazenly in his face.

"I sprained my ankle my first day there," she lied, "and furthermore, my stomach feels none too well from the food. Or water. Whatever." She was prepared to continue the tirade, but he did a quick changeabout and was stamping her in, and she felt an unfamiliar exultation at the thought that she'd done it. She'd successfully brought the film into the country and there'd be no stopping her now. For the first time she understood her siblings' love affair with danger and adventure. She felt nearly six feet tall as she stalked out of the airport in search of a taxi.

Chapter Six

New York was shades of gray: dark gray sky, the rain a lighter gray, the streets a mottled gray; the only discordant notes the occasional striped umbrellas pulled so low their occupants appeared headless. It was oppressively hot despite the thunderstorm, the cab driver was surly, the fare into Manhattan outrageous. And yet Julie couldn't remember ever being happier to see a place.

Her apartment was just as she'd left it—was it only three days ago? It seemed far longer, although even now the events in Athens and Beirut were taking on an aura of fantasy like something culled from a spy thriller. Only her still-bandaged ankle stood as mute testimony that the events of the last few days actually had occurred.

She sat down on the couch to remove the bandages. It was a relief to remove the sweaty material from her ankle. At least the film had been protected by the bandages. And now that she'd brought it safely into the country, what was she to do with it?

Emery had promised to be right behind her, to retrieve it as soon as she'd managed to return, but in the interim she'd do well to hide it, she supposed, the recently learned paranoia returning. And as long as she was paranoid anyway, she got up from the couch and made sure all four locks on her door were in place. She'd never been burgled yet, but this was sure to be the time it would happen. She didn't fancy having to explain to her sister that she'd made it back all right, but then someone had broken into her apartment.

Carrying the film, she went into her small kitchen and almost automatically began to put water on to boil for coffee, then decided she needed sleep more than she needed stimulation. Her eyes lighted on a tin cannister decorated in a watermelon motif and she took it down from the top of the refrigerator. It was halfway filled with David's Cookies, chocolate chip to be exact. She lifted them out, then placed the film in the bottom after having first wrapped it in foil. Putting the cookies back on top, she returned it to its place. Maybe it was an obvious hiding place, but at least the film was protected. And if she was robbed, they'd be looking for money or drugs, wouldn't they? Who'd steal film?

She turned on the air conditioner in her bedroom and, too tired for even a much-needed shower, took off her clothes, letting them drop to the floor in an unaccustomed manner, then climbed beneath the red striped coverlet. She couldn't remember when bed had felt so welcome. She rolled onto her stomach, spreading her arms wide, welcoming sleep, when the phone's jarring ring reminded her too late that she'd promised to call her mother upon her arrival.

The phone rang three times, four times, five. Knowing the futility of trying to blot out the noise, Julie got out of bed and headed for the living room, only to have the phone stop ringing as soon as she lifted the receiver. Getting the dial tone, she punched out the buttons and seconds later her mother's voice was heard.

"It's me, Julie—I'm back."

"Are you calling from the airport?"

"No, I'm at home."

"Julie, I told you to call me from the airport. I thought you could come straight here—"

"Mom, I just wanted to come home and go to bed."

"Your father's back, dear, and we both want to hear what happened. You didn't tell me much when you called and I know he has lots of questions for you."

"Mom, I haven't slept in days."

"You can get a good night's sleep tonight, darling. Right now your father and I are rather anxious to see you."

"Mom, I just got into bed—"

"Would you rather we came to you? We'll just grab a taxi—"

"Never mind, I'll be over."

"You'll stay for dinner, won't you?"

"Only if the food's American," she said, but her mother was speaking right over the words and it was another minute before she was able to get off the phone.

She made a cup of coffee now that caffeine was needed, then took the cup with her into the bathroom and got a shock when she saw her reflection in the mirror. She wasn't sure she'd ever get used to herself as a brunette. She took a long, hot shower, washing her hair in the process, then turned it to cold and stood shivering for a minute or two in the hope that the cold water would revive her. It didn't.

Too late she remembered her hair dryer wasn't in working order, but perhaps it would just look as though she'd been caught in the rain. She didn't want to wait around until it dried naturally. She got into a gray sundress—to match the day—and clear plastic sandals that wouldn't be ruined in the rain. Then she grabbed an umbrella and headed out of the apartment.

A young man shared the elevator with her, one who'd previously exchanged words with her when they met in the building. This time he didn't say anything, just eyed her curiously. Julie knew she should explain the change in her appearance and ease his confusion, but she was too tired and the story would take too long. Actually, he probably wouldn't even believe her. Who would believe that the building's quietest tenant had spent yesterday in Beirut up to her neck in suspenseful living? A few days ago she wouldn't have believed it herself.

Eschewing the subway system for once, Julie grabbed a taxi in front of her building and had to fight to stay awake during the drive to the Upper Westside.

Her mother answered the door, her look of surprise quickly turning to one of disbelief. "Did you decide you preferred to look like your father's side of the family?" she finally asked Julie, clearly feeling insulted that her daughter had chosen to get rid of the one sign of her Norwegian inheritance.

"It was supposed to be a disguise," Julie started to explain, but her mother interrupted her with, "Not now, your father will want to hear about it too."

And then he was there, gathering her in his arms, and Julie realized that she still missed her father's presence. It seemed as though she saw more of him on television than she did in person these days, and the small figure she was used to seeing on the screen now appeared larger than life.

Then her father was offering her a drink which she refused, and her mother was offering her tea, which she accepted, and soon the three of them were seated in the large, old-fashioned kitchen at the round oak table where she'd breakfasted every day as a child.

"Now tell us all about it, Julie," her mother murmured solicitously as though it were a dreaded disease she was going to tell them about, and thirty minutes later she finished relating the events of the last few days, and in the momentary silence her mother got up to make them more tea.

"I'll be damned, so you met up with Noah Majors," were the first words out of her father's mouth.

"Yes, he said he knew you."

"Good man; I'm glad he was there for you."

"I wouldn't say he was exactly 'there for me,'" said Julie, but if she gave herself away by her tone her father hadn't noticed.

"So you have the film, do you? I'd like to take a look at it, did you bring it along?"

That hadn't occurred to her. "No, I hid it in my apartment."

"Very clever of you, dear," said her mother from the direction of the stove.

"Actually I just thought it ought to be protected."

"Quite right," said her father. "Wouldn't want to damage it."

"So Emery's got herself a scoop," said her mother, a pleased expression on her face.

"It's a scoop all right," agreed her father, "but I'd rather she didn't use it."

"All that trouble she went to and you don't want her to use it? Wouldn't you?" Julie asked him.

"Now don't you worry about it, Julie; I'll talk to Emery when she gets back. When is she getting back?"

Julie shrugged. "How would I know? I told you, the last I heard she was being questioned by Mossad." She felt a bit piqued that she'd successfully got the film out of Athens and now her father seemed to want it hushed up.

"I'm sure Emery will see sense," her father began, and her mother continued with, "When did Emery ever see sense, dear, she takes after you."

"It's news, Dad, and the only true account." How could her father not understand when he'd been in the business of reporting all his life?

"Sometimes circumstances dictate that the news is best suppressed," he told her, rather in the manner of God handing down the laws.

"In this country? What happened to freedom of the press?" Julie countered.

"You don't need to concern yourself, honey; I'm sure Emery will understand," he said to her, as usual treating his youngest daughter as though she were still a child.

On the contrary, Julie was certain Emery wouldn't understand, or even listen to her father for that matter, but she was much too tired to argue the point now. She'd done her mother's bidding and gone to Greece; she'd done Emery's bidding and taken the film out of the country; now she wanted to do her own bidding, which was to return home and get some sleep before she collapsed on the kitchen floor of her parents' apartment.

She got up, refused her mother's offer of dinner, once more gave her father a welcome-home hug, then found when she got down to the street that it was rush hour and raining, a deadly combination when it came to finding an available taxi.

Julie headed for the nearest subway station and found, once she'd been squeezed into a crowded car, that men no longer stared at her as they had when she was blond. She'd been undecided before; now she was convinced the new hair color was a bonus. Probably the best thing to have come out of her trip.

With no thought but to get back into bed with dispatch, she unlocked the door to her apartment and stepped inside. Chaos greeted her, a chaos so complete, so extreme, that for a moment she didn't believe the evidence in front of her eyes. The living room had been systematically torn apart. Every book had been removed from the shelves and thrown to the floor; every cushion from couch and chairs had been tossed aside. The drawers to her desk had been taken out, their contents emptied on the floor. A quick glance into the bedroom showed a display of clothes flung around, more drawers emptied, bed linens torn asunder. The myriad contents of her medicine cabinet in the bathroom had been dumped into the sink.

The kitchen she left for last. Something in her wanted to believe it was an ordinary robbery, even though her television was still there, even though her stereo hadn't been taken. But not only was the film gone, they'd taken the entire cannister. They'd even taken her David's Cookies!

Julie's first impulse was to go to bed and forget about it; maybe when she woke up everything would be back to normal. Her second impulse was to sit down on the floor and cry. Remembering she wasn't a crier, she instead reached for the phone, miraculously undamaged, and placed an overseas call to Heracles. Wonder of wonders, he answered on the first ring.

She told him what had happened and there was a long pause.

"Mossad still has your sister in custody, Julie, but I'm sure she'll be released now that they obviously have the film."

"Try to find out, will you, Heracles? Tell her what happened and have her call me as soon as possible."

She thought briefly of calling her local precinct, then discarded it as a bad idea. The already overworked New York police would not be interested in a robbery where nothing was missing but a roll of film. And she didn't want to have to explain to them the importance of that film. She also thought of calling her parents, but her mother would want to send someone over to help her clean up, and her father would probably breathe a sigh of relief that the film was out of his daughter's hands and thus could not now be shown.

She was on her way to the bedroom thinking to hell with the mess, she had to get some sleep, but the sight of her precious books strewn around stopped her. There was just no way she'd be able to sleep if she didn't clean up first. She was a Virgo, after all, and Virgos liked order. Not that she believed in astrology, of course, but still. . .

It was dark by the time the last book was placed in the shelf, the last dress hung on a hanger and returned to her closet, the bed remade and looking inviting. She thought of unplugging the phone so that her sleep wouldn't be interrupted, but then remembered that Emery might call. And damn Emery, anyway, for involving her in the first place in her own questionable escapades.

She hadn't slept more than an hour when the ringing of the telephone woke her up. She saw by her red alarm clock that it was just past midnight, and feeling that it was probably Emery, she got up to answer it.

It was Heracles. "Strange things are happening here, Julie," he began.

"Have you talked to Emery?"

"Yes, she was released earlier after finally confessing to them that you had the film. She made sure you had enough time to get home first, though. But then, when I took her to the airport to return home, she was taken into custody by Mossad again, with the assistance of the Greek police."

"But why? They have the film, what more do they want?"

"I don't know, Julie; I haven't been able to find out anything. Her last words to me were to tell you to carry on."

"Carry on? What am I supposed to carry on with?"

A pause. "Look, Julie, from what I know of your sister, she's every bit as devious as Mossad. I guess you should be prepared for just about anything."

And with those cryptic words, he rung off. Julie just sat there holding the phone. Then, not knowing what else to do, she called her father.

"What is it, Julie? Your mother and I were sleeping."

"Yes, well I've been trying to sleep too, but I think you ought to know that someone broke into my apartment and stole the film and now Emery's in custody again. I think you should get in touch with the State Department or someone, Dad. I think Emery's in over her head this time."

His voice was all concern. "You're right, of course. I'll call a few people in the morning. In the meantime, try to get some sleep, honey."

Try to get some sleep? She had been trying to get some sleep. It was everyone else who was conspiring to deprive her of sleep, not herself. Wondering what could possibly happen next, while at the same time not even wanting to know, she headed back to bed. But now, perversely, sleep wouldn't come. Her big sister, who all her life had managed to involve Julie whenever she was in trouble, had done it once again.

Only this time it was serious, adult trouble rather than childish antics. She felt vulnerable that foreign agents could just freely enter her apartment to conduct a search. And if they were able to take Emery into custody, nothing would stop them from doing the same with her. Perhaps it was all over; perhaps now that they had what they wanted, they'd leave everyone alone. But then why that message from Emery to carry on? Was that supposed to tell her something? Give her a clue? If so, she didn't seem to be able to decipher it. Maybe in the morning. Maybe when her mind was better able to function. Maybe. Then again, maybe not.

Nothing disturbed her sleep until she woke quite naturally close to noon the following day. She got up, used the bathroom, then was on her way through the living room to the kitchen when she noticed the familiar figure slumped down on her couch, sound asleep.

Teddy Bear was back!

Chapter Seven

Julie walked quietly past him on the way to the kitchen, trying not to wake him. He probably hadn't had any more sleep than she the last few days, and at least she'd finally got a few uninterrupted hours and was feeling well rested this morning. She was, in fact, feeling good considering the happenings of late. And it was a beautiful morning, the sun streaming in her kitchen window where she glanced down to see the park filled with people, the usual joggers circling it. Everything seemed back to normal except for the fact that a spy was sleeping in her living room, and even that failed to dismay her.

Julie filled the teakettle with water and put it on the stove to boil, then spooned some instant coffee into two red mugs. He looked so appealing sprawled on her couch, and what's more he was here—here in New York. She didn't doubt that his reason for being here had to do with the missing film, but now that he was here on her own turf she could safely give vent to the feelings she had for him. She wasn't unmindful of the fact that her diaphragm currently resided only steps away.

Also only steps away was the only man who had managed to tempt her out of her self-imposed celibacy of the past few months and the knowledge that she could now go with that temptation made her smile in anticipation. She had thought she'd never see him again, and instead here he was and they were alone and she was sure that something was going to come of it. Something very good, if she wasn't mistaken.

She turned off the burner at the exact moment when it would start the kettle whistling and poured them both coffee. She carried the mugs into the living room and set them side by side on the coffee table, then quietly went into her bedroom to put a cotton wrapper on over her nightgown. She wanted him all right, but there was no sense in being blatant about it. Subtlety, that was the trick.

While there, she straightened up her bed. She didn't completely make it in the event it was soon to be used, but a little straightening wouldn't hurt. She also put a comb through her hair quickly, smiling at her dark-haired image in the mirror. What a happy event it was to wake up in the morning and find the one man in all the world who interested her ensconced on her very own living room couch. Her life was indeed looking up.

Julie sat down in one of the two wingback chairs that faced the couch in a conversational grouping. He looked so peaceful sleeping, almost innocent. Which didn't fool her for a moment. Yasir Arafat no doubt also looked innocent when he slept.

Julie couldn't help noticing how his tan jacket

blended in with the muted browns and beiges in the couch and the way in which his shaggy hair fell down over his forehead as he slept. She had an urge to reach out and push it back out of his eyes, but she wanted to prolong the moment when he'd awaken and they'd be together again. It was more than she had hoped for that he'd suddenly appear like this again. Fate, a propitious fate, must be finally taking a hand in her life. The same propitious fate that had obviously absented itself when her apartment was being burglarized.

But weren't spies supposed to instantly awaken at the slightest noise? She'd been quiet, but not that quiet. Instantly awaken and something else...ah, yes—grab a gun from beneath the pillow. At least in all the books she'd read on the subject the spy always had a gun handy beneath his pillow. She got up and went over to the couch, reaching down between the pillow and the arm. No gun. She reached lower and came up with a dime. But still no gun.

Well, perhaps he was an inept spy, the kind who didn't go by the book. More likely he didn't feel he needed a gun with her. She sat back down in the chair, keeping her eyes on him as she sipped her coffee.

Or maybe that heavy steel watch he wore concealed a weapon. But wouldn't that more likely be a camera than a gun? Or that pen clipped to the pocket of his sport jacket. Perhaps it was a laser-beam pen and right now was aimed at her. And perhaps she was becoming too imaginative by far. He might just be the harmless arms negotiator he passed himself off as.

"Come to any conclusions?" His gray eyes were open now and looking decidedly alert. Alert enough so that he might have been aware all along of her machinations.

"Good morning, Noah. Have a cup of coffee."

He straightened up and grinned at her. "Glad to see me?"

"Thrilled, Noah; absolutely thrilled." She felt a little sarcasm was called for. No sense in instantly throwing herself in his arms. And, after all, his presence had been uninvited.

"Thought you would be." He took a sip of his coffee and grimaced. What had he expected, Turkish coffee? If he didn't like it there were plenty of Greek coffee shops in New York, not that they'd be using anything other than instant.

"It is a mystery to me, though, how people keep finding my apartment when I'm not in the phone book. Am I being followed again?"

He lit a cigarette, then looked around for an ashtray. There were none. She went to the kitchen and came back with a saucer, setting it in front of him.

"Your father gave me your address."

"Thoughtful of him. Did he also give you a set of keys?"

"He didn't need to, the building superintendent let me in."

"I suppose you flashed your ID at him and told him it was government business." The tone was still light but she was annoyed he'd gone through her super, one of the nosiest men she'd ever come across.

Couldn't he have just used the buzzer like an ordinary person?

"Something like that."

"Great. That's just terrific. Now he'll think I'm some kind of criminal. This building belongs to NYU, Noah You could get me in trouble." But she wasn't really taking it that seriously.

"I think you're already in trouble. I understand your place was broken into." He was looking around. "Although it doesn't look like it."

"I cleaned it up."

"Are you always this neat?"

"Always."

"Wouldn't mind having you around. You should see my place in Athens. On second thought, you shouldn't."

"I could tell just by your personal appearance that your apartment'd be a mess."

Noah laughed. "Don't want to move in with me and keep it clean, huh?"

"Afraid not."

"You wouldn't find that a challenge?"

"If I were interested in being a housekeeper, Noah, I wouldn't have gone for my Ph.D."

"It wasn't just housekeeping that I had in mind."

"What *did* you have in mind?" A leading question, but then Julie thought they'd wasted enough time bantering. They had some unfinished business to attend to and she was feeling more in the mood by the minute.

"Later," Noah said, brushing off her question. "Right now there's the matter of the film."

Later? She'd practically offered herself to him and all he could say was "later"? "What film?"

"No more games, Julie—I had a long talk with your father."

Obviously the subject covered was not whether he had her father's permission to pursue her. Miffed by his rejection, she went out to the kitchen for a second cup of coffee. Noah followed her, generally getting in the way. The kitchen was just right for one small person. For one person and another of teddy bear proportions, it was a tight squeeze.

"He's in complete agreement with our government's position on this, you know." Of course she knew. Of all the members of her family, her father was the most supportive of the government, often even when it was wrong.

"Tell me something, Noah. Just what does film have to do with negotiating arms agreements?" The already hot water came to a boil fast and she filled her mug as he looked on.

When he saw she wasn't going to offer him more coffee, he fixed himself a second cup. "I sometimes get other assignments. In this case, since I already knew you..."

"Meaning you'd have some influence over me?"

"I didn't say that."

"I'm sure my father told you the film was stolen."

"Good try, Julie, but it won't wash. We've already found out the film you brought in was a blank. What did you do with the real film?"

"Blank?" It took a moment for the information to sink in.

"And you can forget the look of outraged innocence. I'll admit you had me going for a while there in Athens, but no more. They must be giving courses in deception at NYU these days; you're damn good at it, you know."

Blank film? Her sister had had the nerve to send her back with blank film? Outraged innocence indeed! The truth was, she was madder than hell. How dare Emery perpetrate such a hoax on her? To let her believe she was getting safely out of the country with the film, when all along her ankle was wrapped with some meaningless film, blank at that. And setting her up so that her apartment was searched, especially when her sister knew how she felt about privacy. And now Noah wasn't about to believe anything she said; she could see that by the wary look in his eyes.

"Well? What'd you do with the film in question, Julie?" Patient. Even understanding. Trying, like a good spy, to lull her, she supposed.

"Obviously you're not going to believe anything I say." She stared past him out the window, still fretting about her sister's duplicity.

"I'll believe the real film when I see it. Just give it to me and we'll forget all about Athens."

"I might have lied to you yesterday, Noah—"

"You've lied to me all along. If you don't want to tell me where it is, Julie, I may have to take you in."

"In? In where? I haven't done one thing against the law, Noah—unless lying to spies is some kind of crime!"

"It's not a question of law. It's a question of what's in our best national interest."

"And who decides that?"

He sauntered into the living room and sat back down on the couch, making himself quite at home. "I'll tell you who doesn't decide it, and that's your sister."

She wasn't happy with Emery at the moment, but she was becoming even less happy with Noah. She had thought there'd been some feelings between them, but what kind of feelings could they be if he didn't even trust her? And yet that wasn't really fair. He had trusted her and she'd consistently lied to him. Just as her sister had lied to her.

Julie found she was tired of lying to Noah, deceiving him. He didn't even know how far her deception had gone. She'd lied to him about her personal feelings, too, instead of just being straight and telling him why it was she wouldn't make love. Her feelings of loyalty to her sister were mixed at the moment, but her personal feelings regarding Noah weren't mixed. She liked him. More than liked him, really. She was sure if they could make love together they could resolve their differences afterwards and she'd be able to regain his trust. And along with all that high-sounding justification, she also wanted him, more by the minute.

She sat down beside him on the couch and leaned her head on his shoulder. She could feel him stiffen, obviously wondering what she was up to. "You tired, Noah?"

He made a grunting noise. "You could say that."

"Why don't you come to bed with me and we'll talk about it later?"

"You seducing me, Julie?" Almost indifferent.

"I'm trying to."

"Setting yourself up as some kind of Mata Hari now?"

"Noah—" She saw the dangerous glint in his eyes and didn't plead further. She had a sneaking suspicion her timing hadn't been great.

"Don't 'Noah' me, bitch! And giving your body to me isn't going to get you anywhere. What I can't understand is how a decent man like Johnny could've fathered the two of you!"

He was off the couch and out of her reach or she would've given him a swift kick where it would do the most good. No man had ever called her a bitch before! So much for trying to make it up to him; she'd be damned if he'd ever get another chance. She got to her feet with what she hoped was dignity. "Please leave now, Noah; I have nothing more to say to you. Ever!"

"Did you ever consider going on the stage? You're a born actress, did you know that?"

"Get the hell out of here!"

His eyes were as cold and gray as a December sky. "Not just yet, Julie. I've decided to take you up on your offer."

She glared at him. "Consider the offer rescinded."

"No, I think not." He was moving back towards the couch and she quickly got up and out of his reach.

"Forget it, Noah—it was a mistake."

"Oh, I wouldn't call it a mistake exactly, Julie. After all, I've wanted you since the first moment I saw you. But then I always have had rotten taste when it comes to women; why should this time be an exception?'' He was backing her into the wall and she saw no means of escape.

As he closed in on her she reached for a lamp, thinking to ward him off with it by a quick blow to the head, but his reflexes were in good working order and he grabbed her wrist before she could take hold of it. Pinning both wrists to the wall above her head with one hand, he used the other to pull open her robe. She almost laughed at his look of disappointment. If he'd been expecting a sexy nightgown, he was out of luck. Hers was of white cotton and altogether opaque.

''Don't, Noah—you'll just be sorry if you do.''

''I might be just as sorry if I don't.'' But she could see that the fight was already going out of him, the anger being replaced by a certain sadness.

''Whatever I've done, Noah, is it worth raping me for?''

''I don't consider it rape when you offered to go to bed with me.''

''I'm not offering now.''

He let her hands drop and moved away from her ''I apologize; that was uncalled for on my part. You never really had anything to fear though, Julie; raping women isn't my style.''

''I didn't think it was.'' Softly so as not to incur his wrath again. ''And you might not believe me, but playing Mata Hari isn't my style.''

He gave a bark of laughter that contained no mirth. ''You don't need to tell me; I remember your style quite clearly. It's more like arousing the enemy and then retreating.''

"It wasn't really like that, Noah.''

"Don't tell me what it was like—I was there!''

"Look, this whole thing is ridiculous anyway because I don't have the film.''

"At this point if you said you had it I'd question your veracity. Tell me, Julie, are you really an economist, or was that a lie, too?''

"I think you better go, Noah.''

He didn't give her an argument, just headed for the door. As he opened it, he turned for one parting shot. "If by some remote chance you *are* telling the truth about the film, be careful. You may or may not know it, but you're up against some formidable opponents. And some of them will get a whole lot nastier with you than mere rape.''

She waited until the door slammed behind him, then kicked it with her foot. Since her foot was bare, it did nothing to vent her anger, just hurt instead. That's what came of acting out of character, she supposed, and making the first move in a seduction was definitely out of character for her. But she had seen that after shooting him down twice, he wasn't about to make the first move again, so what was she to do?

If she thought about it realistically it was probably all for the best. He still retained a transient status in her life and she wasn't likely to see him again once the question of who had the film was resolved. It was just that it was difficult to think realistically when her body and mind were in agreement that she wanted him.

Julie went to the front window and pulled aside the curtain to look down at the park. If someone was watching her apartment she'd never be able to tell. The park was filled with all sorts of different people and most of them looked foreign. It was the perfect place for a stakeout as were the crowded streets ideal for following someone.

It unnerved her to realize that some part of her was hoping she was under surveillance, that she risked the chance of being followed if she went out. There was no doubt about it: She had caught the cloak and dagger disease and had readjusted her image of herself from the staid professor to the more colorful one of an elusive character.

She carried the dirty mugs out to the kitchen and washed them, setting them in the drainer to dry. What she felt like was some eggs, maybe some toast, but when she looked in the refrigerator she saw that she was out of eggs, and she knew her bread would be stale by now. Which meant she needed to grocery shop, only shopping for food sounded so mundane. Yesterday she'd been in Greece leading the life of a secret courier; surely today she couldn't go back to being the kind of person who shopped for groceries and cleaned her apartment. Too bad school hadn't started yet; she needed something with which to fill her time. Something interesting. Maybe even exciting. Dangerous? Why not. She'd been to Lebanon, hadn't she, and come out unscathed?

She went to the phone and called her parents. Her father wasn't at home, but her mother had been told to tell Julie that everything was being taken care of, it was now out of her hands.

"What exactly does that mean?" she asked her mother in a disgruntled voice.

"I think it means your father is cooperating with the State Department or the CIA or whomever. At any rate, he said for you not to worry your pretty little head over it."

"He actually said that?"

"You know how your father is, Julie; he still thinks of you as his little girl."

"Well, you can tell him his little girl is not out of it. I just had a visit from his erstwhile friend, Colonel Majors, who seems to think I'm hiding the real film. Where can I get hold of Dad?"

"You can't, darling; he's flown down to Washington for the day. He did say he'd be back for dinner, though. Why don't you eat with us and he can answer all your questions then?"

"All right, expect me." That would at least solve the small problem of having to shop for her dinner.

"Oh, and Julie—"

She'd been about to hang up. "Yes?"

"Wally arrives home today. If only Emery would show up, it would be a real family gathering."

That was good news to Julie. Wally was her favorite, mostly because he was the only member of the family who treated her as an adult. No doubt because he was the only member of the family who was younger than she was.

She made her bed and showered, then was looking through her wardrobe for something vivid to wear that would set off her new hair coloring, when the phone rang. And since she hadn't turned her answering machine on since returning home, it rang and rang. As she'd just spoken to her mother and the school wouldn't be likely to call her in August, she was tempted to just let it ring. But whoever was on the other end of the line had a tenacity that wouldn't let up, and by the thirteenth ring she gave in and picked it up.

She said a curt hello, then listened as an unfamiliar male voice asked whether she was Julia Domino.

"Yes, that's right." Wary.

"Good; I was worried at first when no one answered."

"I was in the shower," she lied.

"I'm awfully sorry—"

"That's all right," she said out of guilt over her lie.

"My name's Bud Corey. I'm a stringer with the *Times* in Beirut and your sister gave me a package to deliver to you. In person, she was very specific about that."

"Emery gave you a package for me?"

"Yes. I saw her briefly in Beirut and when she found I was leaving for the States, she asked me if I'd deliver it. She said you'd know what it was."

Julie knew exactly what it was, and this time she was sure it was the real thing. On the other hand, was this Bud Corey the real thing?

"Are you there?" he was asking.

"Yes, and it's fantastic news. The thing is, how do I know you're really who you say you are?"

"Who else would I be?"

"I'm sorry, but I need some proof."

A silence, then, "Look, do you want to call me back here?"

"If you don't mind."

He gave her a number to call, and when she'd called him back and got the *Times*, her suspicions were allayed. "Sorry about that," she told him, "but I had to be sure. When can I get it?"

"I thought maybe we could meet for lunch."

That was also fantastic news. Her propitious fate seemed still to be at work, this time assuring her of food even when her larder was bare.

"You're on Forty-third Street, right?"

"Right."

"Why don't I meet you up there somewhere?"

"How does Japanese strike you?"

"Anything."

He gave her directions to a Japanese restaurant in his area, then rang off.

Pleased out of all proportion that she was back in the spy business, Julie quickly dressed in faded jeans and a white T-shirt, thinking to blend into the crowd of young people on the village streets. She resurrected a red headband out of her dresser drawer, a souvenir from an aborted flirtation with jogging, and with her wallet and keys stuck in her back pocket, she left her apartment.

She met no one in the elevator and no one in the entry, but she had a feeling her building was being watched. They'd have to be keeping her under surveillance until the film was found.

She ducked out of the building with her head down, then started jogging. All the other joggers were on the other side of the street, using the sidewalk that circled the park, but she headed south for

Fourth Street, circumventing the other pedestrians and wishing she were in better shape. Already she had an ache in her side and her breathing was ragged. Julie glanced behind her to see if someone not in running clothes was also jogging, but didn't see anyone who fit that description. On the other hand, the person following her was probably across the street, and a quick glance over there showed her so many joggers that she hadn't a clue who was legitimate and who wasn't.

She turned right on Fourth Street, slowed down, and headed for the subway entrance on Sixth Avenue. Once there she quickly ran down the stairs, but was slowed down when she had to buy subway tokens. She bought several to have on hand, then headed down to the platform for the Eighth Avenue subway.

Since it was mid-morning the platform wasn't crowded and she positioned herself to watch for others coming down the stairs. The first three people were black, and she quickly discounted them as not being likely to be working for the Israelis. On the other hand, they could be CIA she supposed.

Several young Hispanics carrying large radios followed, then an overweight woman carrying a Bloomingdales's shopping bag. Next several student types, all of whom could be suspect. An A train was pulling in and she got on, staying close to the door. At the last minute before the doors completely shut, she jumped back out, knocking into the woman with the shopping bag.

The woman seemed harassed, but grunted in acknowledgment of Julie's apology. Julie quickly headed for the stairs leading down to the Sixth Avenue subway on the lower level, looking behind her occasionally to see if she was being followed. When she got there a D train was pulling in, and she got on it, taking a seat by the door. She watched the people entering her car but couldn't tell whether she'd seen them before or not.

As luck would have it, the train didn't have air-conditioning and the fans were mostly out of order. Julie could feel the hairband soaking up sweat. She thought it would be not only far more comfortable, but far easier to be a spy in the winter when she could bundle up and not be so easily recognized.

At Thirty-fourth she got off and exited up the stairs leading to Gimbels. She went out the heavy glass doors to the street and headed north to Macy's. Macy's was always more crowded than Gimbels, plus she had a charge account there.

Macy's was blessedly cool after the heat and she walked the length of the store quickly, stopping once at a cosmetics counter to reconnoiter her fellow shoppers. She saw several overweight women, but none of them carried a Bloomingdale's shopping bag, and the only man in the area looked like store security. He was watching her, but she didn't see anything suspicious in that as she was looking around furtively and probably looked like a potential shoplifter.

Julie headed down the few stairs to the men's department and the bank of elevators. One appeared, and she waited until everyone else had entered, then got in and pressed the button for three. Once on three, she went in the direction of her favorite department and saw, with frustration, that the store was filled with winter clothes already, certainly none of which was suitable for the temperature today. She'd really be obvious if she were to leave the store dressed for fall.

In the back of the section was a sales rack and she found a white, cotton Norma Kamali jumpsuit she'd been dying for all summer, and now it was reduced by half. She bought it, and her luck held because the shoe department had a pair of white heels on sale in her size.

Next down to the second floor and the lingerie department. She purchased a bra two cup sizes too large for her, then headed for the ladies' room with her purchases.

She undressed quickly in the small cubicle, putting her old bra and clothes in the shopping bag, then stuffing her new bra with toilet paper until she'd acquired a noticeably larger chest. She waited until she was the only one in the washroom, then left the cubicle and shoved the shopping bag filled with the clothes she'd worn down to the bottom of the trash can.

Surveying herself in the mirror, she smiled in delight. Any man following her would describe her to himself as small and poorly dressed. Certainly he would have noticed a large bust, and that alone should throw him off. She looked taller, far more sophisticated, and sexier than she'd ever dreamed of looking.

Wallet in hand, Julie took the escalator down to

the first floor where she purchased a red canvas shoulder bag and a pair of vividly red sunglasses. A long silk scarf in white, wrapped around her head turban style, added the final touch. When she looked at herself in the mirror, she barely recognized the woman looking back. Surely no one else would recognize her.

She still had an hour before meeting Bud, so she went back to the cosmetics counter and played around with lipsticks until she found one in bright red that seemed to suit her new appearance. The same security man was hanging around, but this time he didn't give her a second look.

She left Macy's and began to walk uptown to the Japanese restaurant. She saw that she was getting chest-level glances from the men on the street, and looked down occasionally to admire her new form. In its way, the stuffed bra was as bad as being blond for walking around New York, she found. Either one seemed to be an eye-catcher when it came to a certain type of man.

She looked around occasionally, but was convinced that she was no longer being followed. She didn't think they'd expect her to be clever enough to change her appearance, and furthermore she hadn't seen anyone who looked in the least familiar.

A block before the restaurant it occurred to her she didn't know how to recognize Bud Corey. And if he was expecting her to look like her sister, he was now out of luck. She could only hope that he had foreseen this circumstance and made a reservation in his name.

The restaurant was cool and dimly lit and she found that Bud had indeed made a reservation but hadn't arrived yet. She glanced at her watch and seeing that she was early, took a seat at the bar. Her feet in the unaccustomed heels were killing her, and a quick glance showed blisters already appearing on her heels. She ordered a gin and tonic and kept her eyes on the door.

In a matter of minutes people on lunch hours began to stream in, and soon she saw one man inquiring of the maitre d' and being pointed in her direction. "Bud Corey?" she asked of him, and he nodded, his eyes taking in her abundant figure.

She put some money on the bar, then followed him to the back where a table was reserved.

"You don't look at all like Emery" were the first words out of his mouth when they were seated.

For her part, he didn't look at all like her idea of a foreign correspondent. His well-tailored suit and silk tie bespoke banking rather than newspapers. He was about her age with an already receding hairline, calm brown eyes and well manicured hands.

"I take after the Italian side of the family," she told him, covering her chest with the menu she'd just been handed. It was getting disconcerting to be constantly stared at below eye level.

"Do you want a drink first?" he asked her.

Julie, who'd brought her drink to the table with her, shook her head. "I'm fine. Except for reading the menu: It's really too dark in here."

He cleared his throat. "Perhaps if you were to remove your sunglasses."

Which, of course, she'd forgotten all about. She slid them up to the top of her head and the printing on the menu popped into view. As did Bud, who now had lost what she'd thought was a fantastic suntan.

She saw him reaching into the inside pocket of his jacket and stopped him with a shake of her head. "Not here," she said in a low voice, looking quickly around.

"I was going to give you the package."

"I know what you were going to give me, but not here. Someone could be watching."

His face blanched. "Don't tell me Emery's into smuggling drugs these days," he said, obviously worried about what he'd innocently brought into the country.

Julie gave him her most reassuring smile. "No, of course not." She looked around. Bud was seated with his back to the door, and anyone seated within viewing distance had already been there when they arrived. "Why don't you put it inside your menu and hand it over to me. Act like you're pointing out something on the menu."

He did what she said, not looking happy about it at all. "Are you sure this isn't—"

"Nothing illegal, I assure you."

"Then why all the secrecy?"

"I can't divulge that information at this time. But you'll be hearing about it soon enough, I expect."

She took the slim package from inside the menu and slipped it into her bag. She kept the red bag in her lap and out of reach of purse snatchers who often operated in crowded Manhattan restaurants during lunch hours.

"What're you having?"

"Sushi," she told him, putting her menu on the table and taking a drink of her gin and tonic.

He gave the order to the waiter, then looked at her again, a full look this time since the menu was no longer shielding her bosom from view.

"I'd be glad to help if you're in any kind of trouble."

"I wouldn't want to involve you, Bud."

"Look, we reporters are used to that kind of thing. Just say the word."

She didn't want help. This was something she wanted to do all by herself. She'd show her father and a few other people that she was someone to reckon with.

"Tell me about Beirut," she said to him, and those turned out to be the magic words. For the rest of their time in the restaurant he told her in detail, rather minute detail, about every minute he'd spent there. Ordinarily she would have found it fascinating. Ordinarily, though, she wasn't herself playing at spy and thus leading enough of a fascinating life of her own that she didn't need to live someone else's vicariously.

He insisted on paying for lunch, and when they parted on the street and he asked for permission to call her, she merely said, "All right, but wait a week or two, would you?" thinking that if things with Noah hadn't progressed in that time she'd give the by now enthralled young reporter a further chance. Only she had a feeling that when he saw how she looked normally, he wouldn't be quite so enthralled.

A quick stop in a drugstore for bandaids for her blistered heels, then she headed uptown: Mata Hari on the move once again.

Chapter Eight

She climbed the stairs to Forty-seventh Street Camera and took a place behind a crowd of voluble people, all waiting their turn at the counter. It was a good fifteen degrees warmer inside the store than out, and Julie could feel the scarf around her head becoming damp and the toilet paper in her bra soaking up the sweat that was starting to run down her chest. While February in New York usually had her looking forward to summer, by August thoughts of relocating in Alaska generally crossed her mind. The only worthwhile thing to do in August was to just sit home in front of an air conditioner and wait for it to pass.

When her turn finally came she took the package out of her bag and opened it. Showing it to the clerk, she said, "I'd like six more just like this."

He gave it a cursory glance before writing up a sales slip and then directing her to the counter where she was to pay. Fifteen minutes later Julie was out of the store, her bag a little heavier and her clothes a little damper.

Now to plant the phony film and throw them off the track. Only she'd already thrown them off the track with her disguise. With a sigh at not having planned her caper very well in advance, she walked back to Macy's with the idea of buying jeans and a T-shirt to replace those worn earlier. But the idea of unnecessarily squandering money assailed her on the escalator, and instead she returned to the ladies' room where she had changed before.

It was a long wait before she got the room to herself, but finally she was able to reach down into the trash can and retrieve the clothing she had discarded earlier. She changed back into her old clothes, putting her new purchases into the now-wrinkled shopping bag, and left the ladies' room just in time. The place was filling up again. Back to her normal appearance, she departed from Macy's and took the subway home. In a perverse sort of way she wished Noah could see what she was up to. It was giving her great pleasure to outspy the spy.

Once in her apartment, she looked around for a suitable hiding place and finally settled on the laundry bag in her closet. They had probably looked there before, but she wouldn't put it past them to do a thorough search again.

Next she made a cup of tea and drank it standing in front of the window in case they'd missed seeing her return to the building. If she hadn't wanted to be followed before, now she desired it. She hoped to leave a trail of phony film to confuse them until Emery returned and took over. Although Julie found she was beginning to hope Emery didn't return all that soon. Playing at being a spy of sorts was becoming second nature to her, and she wasn't that eager, she found, to relinquish the game to her sister.

With the remaining rolls of film and her new clothes packed into a small canvas backpack, she left the apartment once again, this time not even bothering to check out whether she was being followed. She walked the few blocks to the building that housed her office, then let herself into the small room with her key.

This office, which only days ago had been her sanctuary, her retreat from the world, the evidence that she had succeeded in her chosen field, now appeared small and dreary and of no importance to her at all. She couldn't wait to get back out of it and into the real world again.

She looked around and saw the opposition had slipped up somewhere because the room hadn't yet been searched. She put a roll of film in the bottom of her clean wastebasket, then crumpled up some papers and threw them in on top. Next she found a mailing envelope and slipped a roll of film inside, addressing the outside to herself at home. Delighted by the idea, she did it again, this time mailing it to her NYU office.

She left the building, the two mailing envelopes very much in evidence beneath one arm, and went over to Sixth Avenue, walking north until she reached Tenth Street, then turning right to the post office. After mailing both, she went back to Sixth Avenue and stopped in at her bank.

It was almost closing time but the clerk was accommodating and Julie was able to acquire a safe deposit box, wherein she placed the fifth bogus roll of film. The guard then had to let her out the door, which meant no one else could get in until the next day. She figured that'd keep them going for a while. By then she was sure she would have heard from Emery.

She walked further down Sixth and, on an impulse, since it was too early to leave for her parents' apartment, bought a ticket and went into the Waverly Theater. She hadn't noticed the name of the movie on the marquee, and after a half hour of sitting in the darkness she still didn't have a clue what she was seeing. It was blessedly cool, though, and her tired feet were getting a much deserved rest.

When a man who had previously been seated at the end of her row got up and moved so that he was sitting beside her, Julie jumped up and almost ran to the lobby. She had no trouble differentiating between surveillance and hanky panky, and the man had definitely been interested in the latter.

She checked her watch and saw that it was almost time to leave for the Upper Westside. She went into the unoccupied ladies' room and once again changed into her disguise. When she walked out ten minutes later, her chest preceding her by several inches, her backpack now shoved to the bottom of her red bag, she looked and felt like a new person. New enough, in fact, to haughtily throw out her arm to attract a taxi, then sit back in comfort for the ride.

The man who opened the apartment door was almost a stranger to her. Almost, but not quite. It was Wally, but an older looking Wally. A Wally with a full beard and flowing Pancho Villa mustache, a Wally who looked ten times sexier than a brother had a right to look.

She flung herself into his arms, then looked up at him in surprise when he held her off. "It's me, Wally. Didn't you recognize me?"

"Julie?" Still uncertain.

"It's a disguise, isn't it marvelous? And I guess it's good if even you didn't recognize me."

His eyes were on her chest. "A disguise?"

"Yes." She took his arm and urged him into the living room, laughing up at him the whole time.

"It's incredible," Wally was saying, but she was no longer looking at Wally. Nor was she looking at her mother and father, seated side by side on the couch. Instead, she was looking at who was seated in the leather Eames chair, appearing very much at home.

"Didn't I tell you you had a clever daughter?" Noah said to John Domino, and at the words Julie's jubilation subsided.

"What's he doing here?" she demanded to know of her parents.

"Julie, you don't look quite yourself," said her mother.

"I invited him," said her father.

Both parents seemed to have trouble dragging their eyes away from her chest.

"I've been hearing all about your adventures," said Wally. "I'm jealous. They make mine pale in comparison."

Noah merely sat there, a smile of Mona Lisa mystery on his lips.

They all had drinks in their hands, and since no one was offering Julie one, she went over to the sideboard and helped herself to a gin and tonic. Mostly gin. Then she seated herself as far away from Noah as possible and kicked off her shoes. She'd made her grand entrance; now she could be comfortable.

"Delighted to see you again," said Noah, a remark she did her best to ignore.

"Julie, Noah's our guest," her mother remonstrated.

"I understand you're not cooperating with Noah," said her father.

Julie turned to Wally. "You want to go outside and play catch?" It was a codeword from their childhood meaning, let's get away from the grownups and have some fun.

Wally grinned at her. "I'm afraid you're not going to get out of here that easily. You're practically the guest of honor tonight, Julie; we've been awaiting your entrance with baited breath."

"Why the disguise, dear?" her father inquired.

Julie flashed him a look of annoyance. "It's not a disguise."

"Wasn't that what I heard you saying to Wally when you came in?"

"It's not a disguise. I just felt like a change, that's all. To go with my new haircolor."

"You look very. . . arresting," said her mother.

"Thank you. It's a Norma Kamali, I've been wanting it for ages."

Her mother lifted one fair brow.

"The jumpsuit. She's the designer."

"I think we have more important things to discuss than who designed your clothes," said her father, but for once his tone of authority didn't daunt her.

"I have nothing to discuss in front of strangers," said Julie, then heard a noise and turned in time to see Noah choking on his drink. All right, so they weren't strangers. Her family didn't have to know about that.

"But Noah tells us you're not strangers at all," said her mother, leaving Julie to wonder how big a mouth the teddy bear possessed.

They were obviously waiting for her to say something, probably expecting a full confession of some kind, but she sat there, drinking her drink, waiting them out, trying to watch Noah without anyone knowing, particularly Noah, that she was watching him.

Finally her father said, "I was in Washington today, Julie."

"Yes, I know. Mother told me."

"Yes, well, Julie, the fact of the matter is you seem to be making some difficulties for our government. Now you might not be aware of this—"

"I'm aware of it."

"Darling," Julie's mother addressed her husband, "why don't we all go in to dinner. This can wait, can't it?"

"No, Ardith, it can't wait. Time is of the essence here and Noah's come all the way from Athens to get this matter straightened out. The least we can do is accommodate him."

Julie almost laughed out loud at his choice of

words. She'd been quite ready to accommodate Noah only that morning, except at that time Noah had been equating accommodating with compromising. And so instead he had gone behind her back to her father, as though she were a child who still obeyed her parents' every wish. Well, this time she wasn't going to be their obedient little girl. Julie had made a promise to her sister to help, and she wasn't going to go back on it. Forget for the moment that Emery hadn't been completely honest with her. She'd settle that with her sister when she saw her, but until then, she felt just as determined as Emery to see that the film was viewed.

"Noah seems to think you still have the film," her father said to her.

"That's because Noah thinks I'm a liar."

"With some justification, it would seem."

"Dad, I told you the whole story last night. I did have the film but my apartment was broken into and it was stolen. And I don't see how you can blame me for the fact that the film was a blank. You can take that up with Emery."

Her father looked doubtful. "Yes, Julie, I know all that, and when you came in I was at that very moment assuring Noah of those facts. But then you walk in with a disguise, and I must admit that casts some doubt on your story."

"Just because I buy something new to wear, I don't see why you call it a disguise."

In a rather pointed manner, her father's eyes went to her padded chest—followed by her mother's eyes, Wally's eyes, and Noah's eyes—not necessarily in that order.

Julie was feeling on the defensive. "Look, I don't happen to like being followed, all right? So I changed my appearance a little bit, so what?"

"Don't you think you might be getting a trifle paranoid, Julie? What makes you think you're being followed?"

"Ask him if I'm not being followed," she said, pointing her head in the direction of Noah.

All eyes turned to Noah, who shifted uncomfortably in his seat at the cynosure. "We felt it was for her own protection," he admitted, avoiding everyone's eyes.

"Oh, sure," Julie said sarcastically.

"It's very possible members of the PLO are following her," Noah went on.

"See, Julie? It's for your own protection," said her father.

"How do you figure it's for my own protection? I'm not afraid of the PLO."

"Perhaps you ought to be," said her mother. "They are terrorists, after all."

"The ones I met were teenagers."

Now she really had everyone's attention. "Where did you happen to meet them?" Noah asked in a deadly calm voice.

"Never mind."

"It doesn't matter anyway. Your father already told me you were in Lebanon."

"As were you!"

"It was my business to be there."

She gave him a mocking look. "Negotiating arms with the Palestinians now, Colonel Majors?"

"I wish I'd been with you," said Wally, awe in his voice.

"Wally!" their father remonstrated.

"Well, I do," he muttered.

"I really do think all of this can be discussed much more pleasantly over dinner," said her mother, getting up and urging them into the dining room.

Glad of the diversion, Julie followed, and soon they were all in the dining room and taking the seats her mother pointed out to them. Which placed her father at the head of the table, her mother at the foot, Wally across from her, and Noah, unfortunately, at her right side.

One of her mother's law clerks, who made extra money by cooking for her, began to bring in the food. There was salad, there was French bread, but the main course was sushi, no doubt in honor of her father's return from Japan, and Julie involuntarily groaned. "I just had this for lunch," she murmured, then found she had Noah's complete attention.

"I didn't know Macy's had it on their menu," he said to her.

"They don't. I ate at a Japanese restaurant." She turned to her father. "Which proves he was following me or he wouldn't have known about Macy's."

"If it had been me following you, I wouldn't have lost you," Noah said.

She gave him a sidelong glance. "You lost me in Athens. I walked right past you—"

"As a matter of fact, you didn't lose me."

"Don't tell me that. You weren't in Lebanon because you knew I was there."

"Actually, I was."

She turned in her seat to glare at him. "Then back in Athens you knew—you knew all along I'd been lying to you. And you, in turn, lied to me!"

There was a mocking gleam in his eyes. "Spies are often called upon to lie, Julie."

"I don't believe you; you couldn't have known me."

"I wasn't looking at your hair color; I recognized you by your watch."

She looked down at the object in question. "Everyone wears watches like this."

"Not in Greece. And most women don't wear them on the wrist. They wear them further up on their arms, like bracelets."

"You called me a liar, and yet you lied to me all along. What was it you said to me, Noah? That you liked honesty in women, wasn't that it?"

"And I do."

"Then why don't you try being honest yourself?" She was almost shouting before realizing eating had come to a halt while her family avidly listened in on their exchange.

"Julie, why don't you let the man eat?" her mother said at last.

"He doesn't deserve to eat! This man, this dinner guest of yours, has been harassing me ever since I met him."

"Now, Julie—" began her father.

"I mean it." She directed her attention to her father. "Half the spies in the world are following your daughter around, and all you can say is 'Now,

Julie'! Why aren't you helping your daughters instead of cooperating with him?"

"Yeah, Dad," said Wally.

"Wally, stay out of this," warned their father.

"And you—" Julie turned once again to Noah "—if you were so successful in following me, why didn't you just take the film from me in Athens?"

"I would have if I'd known you had it. At that time it was supposed your sister still had it, and since she was in custody . . ."

"You would have taken it? Just like that?"

He nodded, laughter in his eyes.

"That's his job, Julie," said her father.

"His job? I thought protecting American citizens was his job. And since when are you so opposed to freedom of the press, Dad? I would think you'd be fighting to get that film shown!"

"Me too," agreed Wally.

"Generally speaking you'd be right," said her father, "but in this case it's in everyone's best interests that it not be shown."

"It's not in Emery's best interests. Or the Palestinians," added Julie.

"When did you get so political, dear?" asked her mother.

"I'm not political, but I believe in the truth. And the truth just happens to be on that film. And just maybe your attitude is forcing me to become political."

With a sudden show of diplomacy, her father began to talk on what he termed "The Whole Palestinian Situation," and Julie tuned him out. She pushed her food around on her plate, too upset to eat. The one place she felt she'd be supported, and instead her parents seemed to be rallying around Noah. Anyway, as far as she was concerned it wasn't a political matter. It was strictly a family matter. Emery had been lucky enough to get some good film, wanted it shown, and that was that. And if Emery didn't get back to the States soon it would be such old news no one was going to care about seeing it anyway.

Julie was just beginning to cool down when she felt his hand on her leg. Unable to believe what she felt, she looked over at Noah. He was calmly eating away with his right hand, while his left was resting on her thigh. At her parents' dinner table. In front of everyone! She shifted in her seat, but the hand remained in place. She had an urge to shout out, "Look everyone, that spy you're being so nice to is molesting your own daughter under the table," but she didn't. In a funny sort of way she found his hand reassuring. It was as though it were telling her, look, we're in this together, and even though we might be on opposite sides at the moment, the attraction is still there. And she had to admit it was.

Slowly, she began to eat the sushi.

"You don't need to see me home."

"But I insist," said Noah, gaining approving glances from her parents. Her mother had taken her aside only moments before to tell Julie how charming she found Noah Majors.

Nothing had been settled. She thought her parents believed her when she insisted she didn't have the film, but then her parents were used to thinking of her as an honest person, not knowing, as Noah did, what a liar she was becoming. Only out of necessity, though; it certainly wasn't her real nature.

"Lunch tomorrow, Julie?" Wally suggested as she went out the door.

She nodded. "Call me in the morning, Wally."

"I didn't see any sense in taking two cabs since I'd be following you anyway," Noah said to her when they got down to the street.

"I would've taken the subway," Julie said churlishly, but she wasn't actually feeling churlish. From the moment Noah had put his hand on her leg she'd been wondering how she could get him home with her tonight.

He chuckled. "I hear you're pretty agile on the subways."

"You didn't follow me; I would've seen you."

"No, not me."

She turned to him. "Was it an overweight woman with a Bloomingdale's shopping bag?"

He didn't acknowledge her question.

"Was it you dressed up as an overweight woman?"

He laughed out loud. "Only amateurs go in for disguises," he informed her.

"You're lying to me."

He took her arm and put out his other arm for an approaching taxi. "Of course I'm lying to you; it's becoming second nature for both of us, I think."

She waited until they were in the taxi before speaking again. "Are you planning on watching my apartment all night?"

He ignored the question and moved over on the seat so that their thighs were touching.

"What do you do, sit in the park?"

"Actually, I'm beginning to feel like a pariah in the park. As soon as I take a seat, everyone clears off."

"That's because they think you're a cop," she told him.

"Tonight I plan on watching you from a closer vantage point."

His arm was around her now, but she didn't remove it. It felt quite natural there. Rather nice. "Are you going to sit out on my fire escape?"

His lips were on her hair. "Closer than that, Julie."

She felt a ripple of anticipation undulate through her body. "I suppose I'll get up in the morning and find you sleeping on my couch again."

His hand was now moving across her breasts, only she hadn't known it until she looked down. The wads of toilet paper stuck in her bra had prevented her from feeling it. She took the hand and moved it away, conscious that the cab driver could see them in the rear view mirror.

"No, not on your couch," he said.

"Then just where are you planning on spending the night?"

"In your bed, of course," he whispered in her ear, then his lips closed over hers and she was saved from having to make a suitable reply.

Chapter Nine

It seemed that neither of them could wait until they got to her apartment.

As soon as the elevator doors closed on them they were in each other's arms and she was being crushed against his strong body. She lifted her lips for his kiss hoping their mouths would only be used for kissing that night, that the differences between them, the lies, the subterfuge, could be dispensed with for one night so that more important things could occur between them.

The elevator stopped, the doors opened, and they hurried down the hall to her apartment. In her nervousness she fumbled with the keys until he took them out of her hand and tried himself, only he showed his nervousness too, and it was several minutes before all locks were opened and they were inside her hallway.

She turned on the light and a feeling of déjà vu swept over her as she once again surveyed the chaotic condition of her apartment. If anything it looked worse than the first time, as if the searchers were punishing her for having to come back a second time.

"I thought you said you were neat?" Noah asked her with a wry smile, and she leaned back against him and began to laugh helplessly.

His arm went around her. "Hey, I was only kidding. Don't get upset."

She was shaking her head back and forth. "I'm not hysterical, Noah; it's just not the setting I was picturing us together in tonight. I figured they'd—you'd—search again; I just didn't think it would be so soon."

He began moving around, lifting cushions from the floor, straightening lamps. "This wasn't my doing, believe me."

"It really doesn't matter."

"Why don't you fix us some coffee and I'll help you clean up?"

She hadn't planned on spending the evening with Noah straightening up her apartment, but it was early, they had all night. Before going to the kitchen she checked her laundry bag in the bedroom closet. The film was gone. It would only be a short reprieve, however, before they found they once again had blank film.

"What's in the bag?"

She turned to find Noah behind her. "Nothing. Just my laundry."

"You're worried they might have taken your dirty laundry?"

"The film was in there."

His eyes narrowed. "I see. The film you claimed earlier you didn't have you now say was hidden in your laundry bag."

She put a hand on his chest. "Look, Noah, why don't we just take it as an absolute that where the film is concerned, I'm going to lie."

He nodded. "Okay, as long as we also take it as an absolute that as long as I think you're mixed up in this, I'm not going to let you out of my sight."

She smiled. "At least they didn't take the whole bag."

"Why would they want your dirty laundry?"

"Last time they took my cannister of cookies along with the film, but I guess cookies are more tempting than laundry." She gave him a quick hug. "I'll put on some water for coffee." She found that not even having her apartment broken into for a second time could put a dent in her good mood. She and Noah were at last alone together, and for once they weren't fighting. At the moment the only thing that felt important to her was going to bed with him. The hell with the film: She'd worry about that tomorrow.

The cleanup was slower going with Noah helping than it would have been on her own. He was particularly slow in getting the books back on the shelves, pausing every minute or two to ask her if she'd read a particular one.

Julie finally said, "I've read them all, Noah."

"You're kidding!"

"Sure, those and more. I'm a reader; I guess you could say it's my hobby."

"That must make for a sedentary life."

"A quiet life, but it suits me."

"Are you sure about that, Julie?"

She looked over at him. "Am I sure of what?"

"Are you really sure the quiet life suits you? It seems to me you've been thriving on all the excitement in your life lately. You might find when it's all over that the quiet life doesn't suit you anymore."

"What about you?" she countered. "Don't you ever get tired of running around being a spy?"

"An arms negotiator."

"Whatever."

"Never. I think I'd go nuts in a nine to five job. I like the travel, I like each day being different from the one before. Ask your father what it's like—he knows."

"Dad's pretty settled down now."

"Well, maybe when I'm his age. . .."

When the living room was completed, they moved into the bedroom. Here he helped her lift her mattress back up on top of the box springs. The bottom sheet was still on, and she saw no point in making the bed at the moment. Julie ignored the sheets lying on the floor, turned on the air conditioner, then turned off the overhead light and just lit one small lamp on the dresser. Then she turned to him.

"You want to get out of that disguise?" Noah asked her in a low voice.

With a secret smile, she turned to the mirror over her dresser and began to unwind the scarf from around her head. It left her hair flattened down like a sleek cap on her head and she left it that way, liking the look. She could see his reflection in the mirror and he moved fast for such a big man. He was naked and on the bed as she unzipped her jumpsuit and let it fall to the floor.

She felt a twinge of embarrassment while removing her stuffed bra, and indeed he laughed when the wads of toilet paper fell to the floor, but then he said, "I like you better the way you are," and all embarrassment vanished.

Clad only in bikini panties, she went into the bathroom and inserted her diaphragm. She was in a hurry and kept fumbling with it, but finally it was done and she went back to the bedroom. Noah's eyes were closed and at first she thought he'd fallen asleep, but when she joined him on the bed he opened them and said, "It's about time."

"Yes, it is, isn't it?" she replied.

He was reaching out and pulling her close to him. "Is there anything else we have to do before—"

"No, not a thing," she said, closing her eyes and giving herself up to his kisses.

She'd had more expert lovers, men more practiced in the ways of arousing a woman. She'd had one who was a veritable contortionist in bed, but rather than appreciating his facility she'd merely been worn out when he'd finished. What she hadn't had before was a comfortable lover, and Noah was that. He wasn't trying to overwhelm her with passion, nor was he setting forth a bag of tricks with which to awe her. Instead they seemed to meld together as naturally as an act of nature, as though all prior lovers had been practice for the moment when she'd meet Noah and every component would fit together perfectly.

While making love with him, Julie couldn't imagine any other man ever suiting her so well. His kisses were seductive without being sloppy. His hands moved with a swift sureness over her body, not intent on discovering new erogenous zones, but concentrating instead on the tried and true. He didn't rush her, nor did he try to prolong the foreplay to the point where she'd be climbing the walls in frustration. His lips were hungry when they explored her mouth, gentle on her breasts, and inflammatory as they moved down the length of her body.

He entered her at the moment when all parts of her body were perfectly orchestrated, attuned to his in a way they'd never been with any man before. And she yielded, joyfully, overcome by a profound sense of rightness, to the sweeping, primitive, onrushing tide, clinging to him with her hands, her legs and her mouth until something inside her exploded, shattering into separate, exquisite, piercing convulsions.

She caught a look of supreme equanimity on his face when they'd finished, a look that made her laugh out loud in pleasure.

"Are you laughing at me?" he asked her. But she could tell he was only kidding, that he knew she was feeling as satisfyingly content as he was. She moved closer in his arms and fitted her head into the curve of his shoulder.

"It was lovely, Noah. Absolutely lovely."

"It was, wasn't it? You know, I thought it might be like that with you, but then I've thought that before and always been wrong."

Julie knew what he meant. She always entered a sexual relationship with the highest hopes, but until now those hopes had consistently been dashed. And, of course, the expected had happened. She was feeling very much in love, even though she wasn't about to admit it to him. And even though she knew there was no future in it. But love didn't depend on there being a future; it only depended on the right man at the right moment in time, and Noah was that.

"You have two choices, Julie," he said, breaking into her reverie.

Half expecting a proposal of some sort, she eyed him warily. "What are they?"

"Well, we can either eat or we can get some sleep. I don't know about you, but sex always makes me hungry."

"Since all I've had is sushi today, I'm starved," she confessed. "But I'm afraid I don't have any food in the house."

"Any restaurants around open late?"

"There's a Greek coffee shop on Eighth Street."

He groaned.

"But they serve all kinds of food."

He was sitting up in bed. "Great! Lead me to it."

"Tell me, Noah, aren't you afraid of being seen with me? For all intents and purposes, I'm the enemy, aren't I?"

He grinned at her. "Only doing my job. What better way to keep an eye on you than right here in your apartment?"

She dressed in jeans and a T-shirt and smiled to herself as she slung the red canvas bag over her shoulder. She wondered what he'd do if he knew she was walking around with the infamous film in her bag. On the other hand, she didn't think she really wanted to know. She just wanted to enjoy the moment for as long as it lasted.

He left his suit jacket on the chair, but still looked rather formal in pants and a shirt. "Don't you ever wear jeans?" she asked him.

"No."

"Very un-American, Noah."

"I was never a jeans type."

"Not even when you were a kid?"

"I was fat as a kid; I doubt they made them in my size."

She tried to picture him fat but didn't succeed. "Did you have an unhappy childhood?"

"Not unhappy, just fat. I had a mother who equated love with food."

"It seems to have stuck."

"What?"

"Well, you seem to equate sex with food."

He laughed and hugged her to him. "You may have a point there, you know?"

It was after one in the morning, but the streets were still filled with people and the coffee shop had few empty booths. Julie was always surprised to find that at any hour of the night there were always people out in New York. She always assumed that when she went to bed, so did everyone else, but that didn't seem to be the case.

He lit a cigarette when their coffee came and they both ordered eggs and home fries. She wished now she had done some shopping so that she'd be able to make Noah breakfast in the morning. "What happens now?" she asked him.

He reached across the table and took her hand. "You mean after we eat, or with us, or just in general?"

"All three of the above."

"Well, after we eat I figure we'll go back to your place and get some sleep. Among other things."

Noah paused a moment, and Julie nodded in agreement.

"As for us, well I guess that'll take some thinking about. It goes without saying I'm crazy about you—"

"No it doesn't."

"It doesn't?"

She shook her head.

"All right, I'm crazy about you. I'm also crazy about my work, so..." He spread his arms and shrugged.

"Yes. So am I. Crazy about my work, that is."

"And are you also crazy about me?" His face was perfectly, innocuously bland.

"Some of the time."

He seemed satisfied. "Yeah, well that goes without saying. There are times I feel like wringing your neck, you know."

"Okay, and the third part?"

"That's a little more complicated. It'd certainly be easier if you'd stop all the lying and cooperate with me, only I have to admit part of me admires and approves of what you're doing."

"Then why are you trying to stop me?"

"Because it's my job. And because another part of me thinks you're mixed up in something you have no right being mixed up in and you should leave it to the experts to straighten it out."

"Well, I guess two out of three isn't bad."

"What do you mean by that?"

"I mean, Noah, that I didn't like your third answer. All of you in the government might consider yourself experts, but not only do you do the wrong thing half the time, but you do it for the wrong reasons. Furthermore, if we could survive Watergate, I'm sure that Israel can survive a minor embarrassment like this."

"Of course they can, but in this case it's easily circumvented."

"At the expense of my sister's career."

"Julie, your sister isn't an investigative reporter. It was pure luck that she got that footage."

"I don't think governments are going to topple if it's shown. But it will be good for her career. Who knows? Maybe she'll become an investigative reporter."

"No, governments won't topple, you're right. But some fragile negotiations are going on right now and the showing of that film could cause real problems."

"What kind of problems?"

He paused while the waiter set their food in front of them, then continued, "That's something I can't discuss with you."

"You can't or you won't?"

"Both."

"Does my father know about it?"

He nodded.

"And he agrees with you?"

"You know he does."

"Well, I'm sorry, Noah, but I guess one of the things I appreciate most about living in a democracy is having freedom of the press, and I don't like to think that our government has the power to hush things up. If they do, then we might as well be living in Russia or China or any other place where you only learn what the government wants you to learn."

"I don't think it's that bad, Julie."

"Where do you draw the line? If one thing can so easily be hushed up, then so can another, and another, and the system has to become corroded."

"In this case, I really think the end justifies—"

"Don't even say it, Noah. That's the same excuse the communists use."

He sighed. Then, "Eat your eggs, Julie, before they get cold."

They avoided the topic of the film for the rest of their time in the restaurant. Instead he asked her about her work and she told him how she felt about teaching. About her fascination for economics but how she rarely encountered a student who shared that fascination. But when she did, how satisfying it was.

Afterwards they walked through the park holding hands before returning to her apartment. There were still two old men playing a game of chess at a stone table, several people taking their dogs out for the last walk of the day, lovers entwined on park benches and one or two dealers trying to make a sale. There were probably people there to watch her, too, but if Noah recognized them he didn't give any indication. She looked up at her apartment window and saw how well lit it was, how easily she could be seen if she were to stand near the window. She shivered, thinking she'd have to remember to pull down a shade, then led Noah back to the building.

This time he undressed her, but when they were both naked on the bed, she removed his arms from around her and pushed them down at his sides. "This time I want to make love to you, Noah," she told him, stifling his protests by leaning down and covering his mouth with her own.

Julie became intimate with his body in ways still new to her but ones she felt could quickly become a habit if he were to stay around. When she finally lowered herself on to him they both could not wait a second longer, and she rode him joyously, gradually increasing her speed until their separate explosions conjoined and she was left shaken, clinging to his chest.

His fingers were moving through her hair, now curly from the humidity outside. "Such a lot of time we wasted, Julie; if you hadn't tried to be such a cool customer in Athens we might have had this pleasure sooner."

"I wasn't trying to be a cool customer," she murmured.

"Well, whatever you'd call it."

She eyed him speculatively. "I'd call it leaving my diaphragm in New York, Noah."

He looked startled for a second, then burst out laughing. "Hell, Julie, why didn't you just say so?"

She buried her head in his chest. "I didn't know you well enough."

His chest was still moving with laughter. "If you knew me well enough for sex—"

"That's different!"

"I fail to see—"

"Just believe me, it is."

He rolled over, taking her with him, and gave her a kiss on the nose. "Let's take a shower together then get some sleep."

Afterwards, as she was towel-drying her hair, she noticed the traces of black on the towel. Julie saw in the mirror that her hair was getting lighter: Instead of dark brown, it was now several shades lighter and taking on a greenish tinge. She'd have to make up her mind soon whether she wanted to keep it dark or not, and, if so, have it done professionally and permanently.

"Do you like blondes?" she asked Noah when she joined him in bed.

"Sure. I also like brunettes and redheads."

"Did you like me better as a blonde?"

"It was never your hair I went for, Julie."

"What did you go for?"

"Your big mouth. I loved it when you gave me a dressing-down for not looking like your picture of a spy."

She gave him a kiss before rolling onto her side and fitting herself into the curve of his body. "You're still not my picture of a spy," she told him.

His arm went around her and she thought how nice it was to be sharing her bed with a warm, loving man, albeit a spy. Maybe Emery wouldn't return for weeks and weeks and he would stay here with her. She hoped so, because she knew she was going to be desolate when he left.

Bells kept ringing in her dream, then suddenly she was awake and it was the phone. Noah was stirring in his sleep as she got out of bed and went into the living room to answer it.

First she heard static, and then her sister's voice. "Don't say a word, Julie—just listen."

Chapter Ten

Julie glanced at the door to the bedroom. It was open and there was only silence in there, but she couldn't be sure that he was still asleep. And yet if she weren't to say anything, there wouldn't be anything for him to overhear. The only trouble with her not speaking, though, was that there were about a million things she needed to ask Emery, and an imposed silence was effectively tying her hands.

"Think back, Julie," came Emery's familiar voice. "Think back to when we were in high school and I was going with Mark Collier. Remember where I met him. Remember where we used to meet every day. Be there, Julie—this afternoon. And thanks, sweetie."

The line was disconnected so abruptly that Julie stood there for a minute still holding on to the phone. She didn't know whether Emery had been calling from Athens or Beirut or even New York. It was frustrating not to be able to tell her what she'd been going through with the film. Not to be able to tell anyone. The temptation to confide in Noah had been at its greatest point after they'd made love when it hadn't seemed right that she could trust him with her body and not with her mind.

Julie hung up the phone and went over to curl up on the couch and think. Mark Collier; that was certainly a name from the past. Yes, Emery would be sure her sister would remember him. Julie'd had a crush on him a mile long, an unrequited crush, as Mark had only had eyes for Emery.

It had been the summer before her freshman year in high school and her parents had rented a cottage in Long Beach, just half a block from the ocean. It had been Julie who'd met Mark first, proudly bringing him home to show him off to her family. She'd been almost fourteen with no experience with boys. Emery, at sixteen, had been dating successfully since junior high and Julie was no match for her. Mark and Emery had taken one look at each other and Julie, seeing the way things were, quietly bowed out of the running.

She remembered that summer well. When they weren't at the beach, Emery and Mark were sitting around the front porch of the cottage, laughing and whispering to each other and sometimes dancing to the music coming from Mark's transistor radio. Julie tried to stay out of their way and ended up spending the summer with Wally; a brother, however, had not been a satisfactory substitute for a boyfriend.

Julie was sure she could even remember the exact spot where Emery wanted her to meet her in Long Beach. The boardwalk along the beach was lined with eating places and the one frequented most by the

kids during that long ago summer had been the third
one in, the one that sold fifteen different kinds of
knishes. She hadn't been back to Long Beach since;
the following year her father had signed a lucrative
contract with NBC and her parents had bought a
place in the Hamptons which they'd used ever since.

The knish place might not still be there, but whatever was there she was sure that was where Emery
would be. She wondered how she'd manage to rid
herself of Noah in the morning, then came to the
conclusion it wouldn't be necessary. Instead, she'd
get Noah to go to the beach with her and it would be
easy enough to make an excuse and meet her sister.
She'd merely have to say she wanted something to eat
or drink or that she needed to visit the restroom
under the boardwalk.

And he would be a perfect decoy. Anyone watching her would feel confident that as long as she was
with Noah, nothing untoward on her part could take
place. Now she could only hope that it wouldn't rain
or be so overcast he'd be suspicious of her desire to
visit the beach. She got up and looked out the window at the small patch of sky visible from her apartment. It didn't look cloudy and she thought she saw
some stars, but August weather was changeable and
it was hard to be sure.

She trod softly back into the bedroom and quietly
got into bed, curling up her body to conform to
Noah's.

"Who was on the phone?" he asked sleepily.

"My mother, wanting to know if I got home all
right."

"Ummm. Probably Johnny's idea. He undoubtedly thinks I'm up to no good with his daughter."

"Then he's wrong; you were very good indeed," she murmured, and his arms went around her to pull her closer to him. She heard his answering chuckle, then lay quietly and listened as his breathing grew measured, trying to match her breaths to his. Her last conscious thought was that if anyone had ever told her she'd end up falling in love with a spy who resembled a teddy bear, she would have laughed herself silly.

She was awakened by a kiss and opened her eyes to see sunlight streaming into the room and Noah propped up on an elbow, smiling down at her. "You even taste good in the morning," he told her.

She'd been dreaming about him and his kiss had seemed a continuation of that dream. Still not fully awake, she reached up and drew him down to her, feeling somehow snug and safe beneath the weight of his warm body. Her hand burrowed beneath the covers and felt that he was ready, and she shifted her body to accommodate him.

"I'm an old man, Julie; you're going to wear me out."

"I'm sure going to try," she assured him, then gave a deep sigh of pleasure as he entered her and she felt filled, both with him and with her love for him.

Their movements were unhurried as their bodies fell naturally into the rhythms of lovemaking. Their mouths clung together as the languid motions slowly began to ignite their respective bodies and she felt the buildup of dormant passions surfacing, turning her sighs of pleasure to cries of ecstasy as, with each succeeding thrust, she came closer and closer to the moment of fulfillment.

She felt herself reach the peak, then hover for a moment of shimmering intensity before her body became fragmented and her mind became pure sensation. In the moments it took for a semblance of normalcy to return, she wanted to cry out her love for him, to hear the same words from him in return. But only the sounds of their panting breaths filled the silence.

"That's far nicer than waking up to an alarm clock," she said to him when she was able to speak again.

"All you have to do is press my drowse button and we can try it again in another eight minutes."

"Dreamer."

"Not at all; you make me feel like a kid again."

"That's strange, because you make me feel very grown-up."

He gave her a kiss before swinging his legs over the side of the bed, then got up and headed for the bathroom. She stayed still for a few minutes, luxuriating in the warm bed redolent of the smells of his body, the aftermath of love. If it weren't for having to meet Emery, she'd be perfectly content to spend the day in bed with Noah making up for lost time.

He asked if she had a razor, and she found a disposable one for him, then went to the kitchen to put on water for coffee. She was standing at the window drinking her first cup and watching the people in the park when he came up behind her and rubbed his now-smooth jaw against her face. She saw people settling in the grass on blankets and knew it would be a good day for the beach.

"What're you thinking about?" he asked her.

"I was just thinking how long it's been since I've gone to the beach. What're your plans for today, Noah?"

"No plans; just keeping an eye on you, that's all."

She turned into his arms and put her head on his shoulder. "Good; let's go to the beach."

"The beach is for kids."

"Nonsense," Julie argued, although she shared that opinion. She couldn't remember going to the beach once since she'd graduated from college.

"I can't go anyway—I don't have a bathing suit."

"We'll buy you one." She moved from his arms and handed him his cup of coffee. "But first we'll go out to breakfast."

"I would have bet you'd be the type to fix me breakfast."

"And you'd be right, but today I happen to be out of food."

Julie carried her cup of coffee into the bathroom and took a shower. As long as the razor was already out, she decided to add some class to her act and shave her legs. When she emerged from the shower, she noticed that her hair was getting lighter with each washing. She was afraid the sun and the salt water at the beach might combine to either turn it back to its natural blond or render it some disastrous shade of olive green. Some kind of head covering might be in order.

Noah eyed her appreciatively as she put on the bikini she found in the back of her drawer. Over this she donned white cotton pants with a drawstring waist and a billowing shirt in a vivid shade of turquoise. She fastened a straw hat on her head and shoved two large bath towels into her canvas bag.

Noah left his jacket and tie off, but with his dress shirt and leather shoes he looked far too formal for the beach. Perhaps she could persuade him to invest in an entire outfit.

She took him to Jimmy Day's on Fourth Street for the biggest breakfast she'd eaten in years, then over to Christopher Street to look in the men's shops for a bathing suit. The stores were showing suits for men that were smaller than the bottom of her own bikini, and Noah refused to even consider them.

"No way am I going to parade around in something like that looking like a—"

"Noah!" she cut him off, mindful of the fact the effeminate clerk was within hearing distance. Noah hadn't even noticed that the salesmen in the shops had been ignoring Julie and honing in on him.

"We'll go to Macy's," she told him when they got out of the shop. "It's right near the railroad station anyway, and I'm sure they'll have something you like."

On the subway ride uptown he started to argue that he didn't have enough money with him for unnecessary purchases, but Julie assured him that Macy's would be happy to honor the American Express card he admitted to having.

Noah found a pair of trunks at Macy's that suited

him. They were navy blue, baggy and hit him at the top of his thigh. Julie thought them unaesthetic, but didn't mention it for fear he'd refuse to go at all. With a little subtle urging from Julie, by the time they left the store he was wearing white duck pants with an elasticized waist, a navy blue knit shirt sporting an alligator over the pocket, and tennis shoes so new and white they looked almost obscene out on the dirty sidewalk.

Julie thought he looked terrific. She took his hand and led him through the crowds to Penn Station where they bought a *Times* before boarding the train for Long Beach.

They shared the newspaper on the train. Julie read the financial section while Noah skimmed the others, and in less than an hour they were in Long Beach and standing in line to get their beach passes.

"This doesn't look much like a beach town," Noah noted, looking around.

"Maybe not, but it is. Wait'll you see the beach—you'll love it."

He muttered something darkly that she took to mean he wasn't about to love any beach, but might consent to like it a little bit if forced.

Hand in hand they walked to the beach and when they turned onto the boardwalk, Julie gave a surreptitious glance inside the knish place. No Emery yet, but it was still early. She was surprised to see how little the place had changed. There were a couple of new apartment buildings fronting the beach and one of the former eating places now had only electronic games, but other than that it was the same.

They found an uncrowded spot on the sand where Julie spread out the two towels before heading towards the water. Noah, she saw, wasn't going to have any part of the water but was instead settling himself on one of the towels. Except for his forearms and face, he lacked any color. She hoped he wouldn't plead sunburn and want to leave before Emery had a chance to arrive.

The water was refreshingly cold and she swam out beyond the breakers and floated for a while before joining Noah on the beach. She shoved her wet hair up under her straw hat and settled down on her stomach.

The first hour passed with desultory conversation on how they'd spent their summers as children. She learned that Noah was from a small town outside of Madison, Wisconsin, and while there had been plenty of lakes nearby, he'd used them for purposes of fishing more than swimming. Julie, who'd never been fishing, thought it sounded boring.

She asked him about the Greek islands and he told her that he'd never been to any of them, preferring to remain in Athens. She brought up baseball and discovered he hated it, preferring football. Julie loathed football. She started a discussion on movies and found that his idea of a superb film starred either Clint Eastwood or Charles Bronson; she preferred the more sensitive films coming out of France. Any discussion of music came to a halt when she discerned his idea of good music was the kind played in elevators in New York.

"How about books?" she asked.

"I don't have time to read," he answered, leaving her to wonder what he did in his spare time besides going dancing at the Hilton.

"You know, Noah, I have a feeling we have very little in common."

"Yeah, isn't it great?" And he did sound enthusiastic about the news.

"What's so great about having nothing in common?"

"Listen, my wife and I had everything in common, and it turned into a disaster."

Having run out of conversational gambits, Julie suggested she go up and get them something to drink.

"I'll go with you," he offered.

"You don't need to; just tell me what you want."

"Do they have beer up there?"

She nodded.

"Get me a couple."

"Two?"

"Why not;' it'll save you another trip."

Julie declined his offer of money and picked up her red bag before walking up the beach to the boardwalk. She went straight to the knish place, but Emery had not yet arrived. She didn't think she'd be able to carry three drinks, so just bought two beers. When he was ready for a second it would give her an excuse to return once again.

She glanced into each open food stand as she walked the length of the boardwalk. She could have been wrong about which one Emery had in mind. The way she remembered it it would have been the knish stand, but her sister could be thinking of an entirely different one.

There was no Emery. There were some suspicious looking characters, but no more suspicious than she saw every day on the city streets or in the subways. She realized that while she was still a people watcher, it now had paranoiac overtones to it.

Before getting in line to order the beer, she pulled both packages of film out of her bag, ascertained which was the film her sister had used, and put it in the center, zippered compartment of the bag. The other she left in the section housing her wallet and cosmetics bag.

Noah's countenance lit up considerably when she handed him the beer. He wasn't actively grumbling, but he didn't appear to be enjoying his day at the beach as much as she was. And she was enjoying it, she found. It felt good to get out of the city and breathe some fresh air and feel the cooling ocean breeze, and she had forgotten how much she liked to swim.

A couple to the right of them was tossing a frisbee back and forth and Julie thought of buying one for the next time. Just lying in the sand became somewhat monotonous, but if she and Noah had something to do... It was with a pang that she realized there wouldn't be a next time. Emery would pick up the film today and no doubt get it shown soon after. And that would be the end of it. Noah would return to Athens and Julie would return to normal.

"Why the stricken look all of a sudden?" Noah asked her.

"Oh, nothing," she said, brushing his question aside. More lies to him; she'd be glad when that aspect came to an end.

"I'd love to know what's going through that devious mind of yours."

"Devious?"

"Yes, devious. You think I don't know you're just waiting for the next event to take place? What's it going to be this time? Are you going to change into a mermaid disguise and disappear into the sea?"

She managed a laugh. "What would you do if I did?"

He eyed her speculatively over his beer. "Oh, I don't know. Maybe change into my shark disguise and go after you."

"Do you really see hidden motives in everything I do?"

"Maybe not everything, but I did wonder why you wanted to get me out of the city today."

She began to trace a pattern on his chest with her hand. "I honestly didn't have a motive, Noah; I just thought it would be more pleasant than sitting around my apartment all day."

"You're sure it had nothing to do with that middle-of-the-night phone call you got?"

"Cross my heart," she said, making the gesture and hoping he believed her. And yet he must have reached the point by now where he mentally questioned everything she said.

He stopped her hand in its movements across his chest and held it. "Don't you think we ought to have a serious talk, Julie?"

That was the last thing in the world she thought they should have at the moment. "Can't we just enjoy the day at the beach, Noah? Couldn't we pretend, for just a few hours, that we're no different from the other couples here?"

The look he gave her was enigmatic. "I'd prefer a little honesty."

She pulled her hand away from him and sat up. "If you liked honesty so much, you wouldn't be a spy!"

He chuckled. "If it fits some romantic image of yours to think of me as a spy, far be it for me to disabuse you of the notion."

"I don't see you negotiating any arms deals."

"You just happened to meet me—"

"At the wrong time?"

"Putting words in my mouth again? I was just going to say—"

She put her hand over his mouth. "No more lies, Noah; I don't think I can take any more lies."

He kissed the palm of her hand before moving it away. "Beautifully rendered, Julie; you're really getting expert at subterfuge. I'm beginning to wonder why you aren't the one filming documentaries and your sister isn't the economist."

She got to her feet and headed for the water. "Going to cool off?" his mocking words followed her.

He could truly be infuriating without much effort at all. She'd been sincere when she'd said no more lies, but it was fast reaching the point where if she told him the sky was blue he'd no doubt question it.

Julie swam out past the breakers and then headed,

in even strokes, parallel to the beach. She thought of emerging from the water at a point further down the beach and checking to see if Emery had arrived yet. But then she remembered her bag containing the film was on the beach. For that matter, Noah might be watching her.

She swam until she began to tire, then once again joined him on the sand. She shook the water out of her hair and told him she was going up to the boardwalk to use the restroom. "Do you want another beer while I'm up there?"

"I can get it myself."

"I'll be going right by there anyway."

"All right, but this round's on me. I insist."

She took the proffered money and dropped it into her bag. In case he happened to be watching, she visited the restroom beneath the boardwalk first, but it was so damp and dank she didn't linger there for long.

Again she didn't see Emery in the knish place. She stood in line for the beer, adding a couple of hotdogs to the order, and when she'd paid and had turned around, a voice called out, "Over here, Julie."

She looked to her left and saw Emery seated at one of the metal tables. Trying not to show any surprise, Julie casually walked over to the table and set one of the hotdogs and a container of beer down in front of her sister, then took a seat across from her.

"For me?" Emery said with a smile. She took a bite of the hotdog as though it were just any ordinary day at the beach.

"Noah's here with me, Emery."

A raised brow. "Noah? A boyfriend, Julie?"

Julie shook her head. "Colonel Majors. Of the CIA."

"Really, darling, do you think that was wise?"

"I had no choice, Emery. It was a question of either bringing him with me or being followed."

"You're doing well, sweetie; I meant to tell you."

"Emery, what happens now? What're you going to do with the film?"

"You have it with you?"

Julie nodded.

"I'm going to take it to London, to the BBC. A friend of mine there, Harry Blake, will get it shown."

"Why not here?"

She gave a wry smile. "I'm afraid they're not going to let me."

"How about Dad? Wouldn't he help you?"

"Surely you know his position on this by now."

"But if you talked to him, Emery—" She broke off at the expression on her sister's face. She was looking over Julie's head at something behind her.

"It's the Israelis, Julie," she said in a low voice. "Get out of here fast. I'll try to delay them."

"I've got a better idea," Julie said quickly, reaching into her bag for the last roll of phony film and handing it openly to her sister. "Can they hear me?"

Emery's eyes widened at the sight of the film. "No," she said, without moving her lips.

"This isn't the real film," Julie assured her quietly. "Don't worry, I'll get the other to London for you, I promise."

As if summoned up by a magician, Yotav materialized by Julie's side. His eyes, however, were on Emery.

"I'll take that now, Ms. Domino," he said, and Julie could have sworn he was relishing the moment unduly. And yet maybe not unduly; her sister had evidently been leading him a dance.

With a quick gesture, Emery shoved the film down the front of her shirt, just as obviously relishing her own moment. Her eyes were sparkling as she glanced up at the Israeli.

"That's hardly going to change the outcome," Yotav warned her.

"You try anything and I'll scream so loud half the beach will come running," hissed Emery, as Julie silently applauded her.

Yotav looked amused. "In New York? I think not. I could probably kidnap you right now and no one would interfere."

Before Julie knew what was happening, her sister was on her feet and running out the front of the restaurant, Yotav following.

Julie ran outside and watched as her sister raced down the boardwalk, then leaned over in time to see Emery disappear into the women's restroom and Yotav come to a precipitous halt just outside the entrance. She was debating whether to go after her or to get out of there before they found out that once again they were after the wrong film when she saw a movement at her side and looked around to see Noah beside her.

"I got tired of waiting for that beer."

Coming up behind Noah was Yotav and two other

men, all of them looking incongruous on the beach in their summer suits. She should have left while she had the chance. As it was, she'd have to return to the apartment for clothes and her passport and she didn't know how long Emery would be able to hold them off. She didn't think a little thing like a "Ladies" sign would deter Yotav and his men from entering the restroom and forcibly taking the film from Emery.

"Taking the sun?" Yotav asked Noah.

Noah looked nonplussed at being found wearing a bathing suit on the job. "Where is she?" he asked the Israeli.

Yotav pointed in the direction of the restroom. "You want to be in on it, Noah?"

Julie waited for Noah to refuse, but he merely grinned. "Wouldn't miss it for the world."

Julie's eyes narrowed as she looked from Yotav to Noah. "You set me up," she accused him.

Noah shrugged. "What did you expect?"

"It was all a setup? All of it?" Even the sex? she wanted to add, but desisted in the presence of the built-in audience. She heard Yotav laugh and turned to glare at him.

"You aren't the first woman he's fooled," the Israeli told her, and when she looked back at Noah he wouldn't meet her eyes.

"Better run along, Julie," Noah said to her, as though telling a child to get lost.

"Go on," he reiterated when she didn't move. "Your sister will be all right. Nothing's going to happen to her as long as she hands over the film. And she will, you can be sure of that."

"You bastard," she said to him, the unfamiliar word coming naturally to her lips.

Noah gave an indifferent shrug and turned back to Yotav. Without giving him another glance, Julie ran back onto the beach to get her clothes. She put them on, then shook out the towels before shoving them into her bag. She had somehow believed that when it actually came down to it, Noah would help her. She was the American, wasn't she? and she was the one in the right. To say nothing of the fact that they'd spent the night in each other's arms.

With a small show of defiance, Julie kicked sand all over Noah's clothes before turning to leave the beach.

Back at the train station she couldn't find a taxi that would make the trip into Manhattan, and having fifteen minutes before the train was to leave, she located a phone booth and called Wally. Luckily he was at home.

"I thought we were going to have lunch today?" he asked her.

"Never mind that, Wally—I need your help."

"Ask away."

"And listen, this is just between us. Don't tell the folks."

"Understood. Just tell me what you want, Julie."

"Two things. A blond wig and some of your clothes. I need to look like a boy for a short time, Wally. Do you think you can do that and meet me at my apartment?"

"No sweat, I'll see you there."

"I'll be coming in from Long Beach on the train, so if I'm not yet there when you arrive, wait."

She kept a watchful eye out, but by the time the train pulled in she still had seen no sign of the Israelis or Noah or Emery. She'd bet on her sister's being able to successfully hold them off until she thought Julie had enough time to get out of the country.

Julie's only regret was not having buried Noah's clothes in the sand so that he'd have to go burrowing for them like the rat he turned out to be.

Chapter Eleven

"No, Julie, that won't do at all! You're not walking like a boy."

Julie gave him a look of exasperation. She had little more than an hour to get to the airport in order to make her flight to London, and Wally was more concerned over whether she could walk like a boy than whether she'd get there on time.

"All right, Wally—show me how a boy walks."

He'd brought her his Little League outfit from years before and although she'd rejected it out of hand, he'd convinced her to at least give it a try. It had fit all right and she did feel her face, bereft of makeup, looked like that of a boy beneath the baseball cap.

Wally, however, had pointed out that it wouldn't do—her chest protruded. Which had led to his ripping up one of her good sheets and wrapping it, mummylike, around her chest until her contours indeed looked flat beneath the loose shirt. And who cared anyway if she didn't walk like a boy? If she looked like one, who would question it?

"Boys walk all different ways and it's not as though I wiggle my hips, Wally; I have a very straightforward walk; I'd even go so far as to describe it as a unisex walk."

Wally was hunched over in the chair and looked doubtful. "But kids don't walk like that. And what's the sense in getting up that disguise if your walk's going to give you away."

"Well, how do they walk? You seem to be the expert, show me how."

He seemed to be considering it. "I think the best thing would be for you to strut. Picture yourself as a cocky street kid with a big mouth."

"You mean like Emery when she was a kid?"

"Exactly!" They both smiled at the recollection. Emery, who'd always been small and deceptively fragile looking, had been the terror of their neighborhood when they'd been kids.

"Wally, I've got to get on a plane in this outfit."

"Just try it, Julie."

She shoved her hands into her pockets and began strutting around the room, imitating the way she recalled Emery had walked when they'd gone to school together. She was followed by Wally who seemed intent on studying the movement of her hips.

"Here, carry this," he said, handing her a well-worn baseball glove.

She put it on her left hand and with her right started pounding the pocket. "This is ridiculous, Wally."

"No it's not." He sounded exultant. "That's it, I think you've got it!"

"You sound exactly like Henry Higgins."

"I feel like Henry Higgins."

"Fine. Now let me see the wig."

Wally produced a shopping bag, pulling a long, blond wig out of its depths. Julie could see that the flowing hair would reach at least to her waist.

"You've got to be kidding. Didn't they have anything shorter?"

"You don't like it?"

"It's a bit much. I'm going to look like Lady Godiva or something."

"You just said blond, and this one was on sale."

"All right, I guess it'll do."

"You don't like it."

"It's fine, Wally, and I really appreciate your help. And look, don't get excited, but I'm going to have to ask you to shave off your beard and mustache."

Wally balked. "Listen, Julie—"

"I wouldn't ask you, Wally, if it wasn't absolutely necessary."

"Convince me."

"You have to pass as me."

"You convinced me. Only Julie—one little detail— how do you propose making me a foot shorter?"

She grabbed him by the hand. "Come on, I'll explain it to you while you're shaving."

In the bedroom, Wally took one look at the unmade bed, then did a doubletake. "How come your bed's not made, Julie?"

Leave it to eagle-eyed Wally to notice that "Because it just isn't, that's why."

"I've never known you not to make your bed."

"Come on, Wally, am I *that* predictable?"

"I always thought so."

"Well, I guess I'm changing," she said, disgusted herself by the image she had been projecting all these years.

"Whose jacket is that?" Now he'd spotted Noah's jacket, left behind when they'd gone to the beach.

"None of your business," she told him.

"I'll bet it's that agent's—the one you left with the other night. What was his name, Noah?"

She nodded.

"You two going together?"

"No, Wally. In fact at the moment, we're not even speaking."

And then he just wouldn't quit questioning her until he'd got the whole story out of her, somewhat censored, of course. It wasn't really necessary for Wally to know every last detail of her life.

"And he was one of Dad's friends? Dad'll kill him for this, you know."

"Wally, I told you this in confidence."

"Then *I'll* kill him."

"Spare me your theatrics, Wally, and start shaving. There's a razor in the bathroom."

"*My* theatrics? Who's the one dressed up like a boy?" He did go into the bathroom, though, and seconds later was demanding a new razor. "This one won't cut anything," he complained.

She found an unused disposable razor and handed it to him along with scissors, all the while admiring her new look in the mirror. It was amazing how many new looks she'd acquired in just days. From blond to brunette, from a bra stuffed with toilet paper to her

new, flattened shape. And there was the long blond
wig to look forward to.

"Could I please hear the reason for this?" he
asked her. "It took me all summer to grow this
beard."

"You're my decoy, Wally. All you have to do is
stand in front of the window occasionally, maybe
walk back and forth. And anyone watching from the
park will think it's me."

"I could even stick my head out once in a while
and yell down at the street."

"Don't overdo it, Wally. Just seeing you ought to
be enough."

"And I have to do this the entire time you're flying
to London?"

"Would you mind?"

"No, I'll just sit around and watch the game on
TV. You got any food in the house?"

"Sorry, I'm afraid not. But you can order some
in."

"No food? You really have changed, Julie."

"Well, it's only temporary," she muttered, leaving
the bathroom and getting Wally's athletic bag from
the living room. He used it to transport his baseball
uniform, and she thought she'd carry it with her to
London. It looked like exactly the sort of thing a boy
would carry.

She put the wig inside and added a dress, a pair of
sandals and her makeup kit. Then, realizing a boy
wouldn't be carrying a purse, she also added the film,
her wallet and her passport. She looked at her watch,
saw that she had to get going, then also put her watch

into the bag. It could conceivably pass as a boy's watch, but she wasn't going to take any chances.

"Hurry up, Wally," she called to him.

A minute later he emerged from the bathroom sans facial hair. She handed him a pink T-shirt and insisted he put it on.

"But you wear white T-shirts, Julie," he protested.

"Please, Wally, just do as I say. In fact I think you're going to have to wear a bra."

"Oh, come on, Julie—you're not all that big."

"Big enough you had to strap me in, if you recall!"

They found, however, that the bra wouldn't reach around his back, but she finally found a tube top that stretched to fit him, and they managed some wads of toilet paper strategically placed that ought to fool a watcher from a distance.

"You look adorable, Wally," were her parting words, then got out the door before he could change his mind. He was standing at the window when she left, and she was sure any watcher in the park wouldn't bother with a little boy coming out of the building when their quarry was plainly in view.

On the street she longed to look up and see what picture he presented, but she didn't dare. She took off down the street, nylon bag in one hand and a baseball glove in the other. Occasionally she reached up and rubbed her nose with her knuckles, something she'd noticed boys often did, and when she got to the corner she hailed a cab.

The cab driver was initially reluctant to transport a

child to the airport, but when she paid him in advance, he took off in a hurry.

"You running away from home, kid?" she was asked.

Julie lowered her voice to answer, "Nah, I'm just meeting my parents."

"You play ball?"

"Yeah." Just her luck to get a talkative cabby.

"What position you play, kid?"

"Catcher."

"Yeah? Then how come you're carrying an outfielder's glove?"

"What's it to you, mister?"

She received an annoyed glance via the rearview mirror. "Just trying to be friendly, that's all."

"I was playing catch in the park, that's why."

The rest of the ride the driver discoursed on the Mets' pennant chances, and Julie didn't bother telling him she was a Yankee fan. She decided that wouldn't be politic if she wanted to arrive at JFK alive. Mets' fans were known to get carried away.

She'd made a reservation in the name of Jules Domino and hoped no one at the airport would give her a hard time about traveling alone. But when she was asked, she claimed to be fourteen, and the ticket clerk seemed to accept that. She figured there were plenty of fourteen-year-old boys who weren't any larger than she was.

Her seat partner was a dark-skinned young man who gave her a couple of strange looks. Julie hoped he wasn't one of those types who went for little boys. When she forgot herself and ordered a gin and tonic from the flight attendant, then quickly switched to Coke when told she wasn't old enough to drink, the young man beside her made a choking sound. She turned to see him convulsed in laughter.

"So I drink, so what?" Julie growled. "A lot of kids my age smoke dope."

The man reached over and covered Julie's hand with his, causing her to snatch it away as though burned. Oh no, he *was* one of those! Well, he couldn't very well molest her on the plane, could he? If he even tried she'd call for the flight attendant and make a fuss.

"It's okay," he said, after having to control his laughter once more. "I'm a friend of your sister."

"I don't have a sister." Not that he didn't look Emery's type. Emery's type seemed to be anything foreign.

"My name is Mustafa and I'm your friend."

She seemed to be acquiring a lot of friends lately. More than she wanted. "What kind of name is that?"

"It's Arab."

"Yeah? I never saw an Arab in person before. How come you're not wearing one of those robes? You a millionaire?"

He ignored her childish questions. "I assume you have the film with you."

Knowing about the film didn't prove anything. It was more likely he was one of Yotav's men and the ruse with Wally hadn't worked at all. She ignored him, wishing she had something a little stronger than Coke to drink.

"I will prove to you who I am," he said in a low voice. "You are carrying the film of the hijacking, am I right?"

"I'm afraid that doesn't prove anything," she told him.

"Ah, you think I am Mossad."

"What's Mossad?" Julie asked innocently in her little boy voice.

"I can only tell you that your sister was taking the film to the BBC to be shown. When we saw her picked up at the beach by Mossad, we watched every plane taking off for London until we spotted you."

"You mean you knew who I was?"

"Not at first. There was a resemblance, but we weren't certain until we checked your name against the manifest. It was too close to be a coincidence."

"You could still be Mossad."

He sighed and began drumming his fingertips together. "I'm a friend of Mohammed, your sister's lover."

"Mossad could know about that."

He reached inside his back pocket and pulled out a passport, handing it to her. It was Jordanian, but that still didn't prove anything. She was sure spies had all kinds of phony passports. She'd even had one herself in Greece.

"I'm afraid that still doesn't convince me."

"Shall I recite the Koran to you?"

She laughed. "Since I don't know it, you could be reciting anything. Tell me something Mossad couldn't possibly know."

"I know your sister sent the film over with a *Times*

correspondent, but perhaps Mossad was aware of that.''

Julie reached over and patted his hand this time. "Very good. I don't think they do know about that.''

"Then you believe me?" Mustafa's relief was evident.

"Maybe, but I don't trust you. I can take care of this myself; I don't need you along.''

"You'll need some place to stay. They'll be checking the hotels.''

"I'm going straight to the BBC offices.''

"In the middle of the night?''

Julie shrugged. She hadn't had time to really think it through. Hotels were out, though, for obvious reasons. Perhaps she'd just hang around the airport until business hours and then try to contact Harry Blake.

"When this is all over, your sister is going to do a documentary on the camps.''

"I'll bet she is.''

"Have you ever seen one of our camps?''

Julie shook her head. "I've seen pictures, though.''

"I was born in one.''

Julie looked at him closely for the first time. He couldn't be more than twenty or twenty-one, younger than Wally, she thought, and far too young to be in the kind of business he was in. "Tell me about it.''

If the information about the *Times* correspondent hadn't convinced her, the story of his life would have. He put in too many realistic details not to believe that he'd actually been brought up in a camp.

The living conditions had been horrendous, but there'd been money to educate the youths, and he had been attending a small college in South Carolina for the past year.

"How did you get mixed up with the PLO?"

He gestured with his hands expressively. "They are our only hope; the only ones who care whether or not we rot in those camps forever. And they pay for our education."

"But couldn't you live in Jordan?"

"Sure. And you could live in Canada. But do you choose to?"

"I don't know," Julie told him. "I can't say I much like Mossad's role in this thing with the film, but I've got to say I support Israel's right to a secure country. And at least the Israelis aren't usually the ones running around hijacking planes."

"We don't hate the Israelis; they are our cousins. But our families lived there too, for thousands of years. We just want to be able to return home and live in peace."

"Well, I hope you get your wish some day," she told him, not feeling able, at the moment, to single-handedly solve the problems in the Middle East.

Julie couldn't even solve her own more immediate problem of how she felt about having gone to bed with a man who'd set her up and then quickly dumped her when he'd got what he was looking for. Meaning the film, of course, not the sex. She'd wondered at the time why he'd come on to her so strong so early, not quite trusting that it was due to any personal charm on her part. And she, fool that she was, had fallen for him.

Not that she couldn't be reading things wrong. There was always the slight possibility that he'd been playing a part at the beach, trying to act as though he didn't care in order to get her out of Yotav's reach. Except she couldn't see any reason for that. After all, he hadn't known she still had the film.

It was just unfortunate that she couldn't seem to turn off her emotions with the same facility as Noah. She still loved him, with the added emotion of hate now thrown in. Well, it was probably what she deserved for being so lacking in class that she'd fallen for a spy to begin with. Spies were notorious for being rogues, after all.

Julie was happy to see dinner arriving down the aisles and remembered she hadn't even eaten her hotdog at the beach. Her seat partner claimed not to be hungry, so she finished off his tray, too, then settled back in her seat to watch the movie. It didn't sound like the kind of film she enjoyed, but she hadn't brought along anything to read and she didn't feel up to more conversation. Talking like a little boy was giving her a sore throat.

It was one of those silly *Star Wars* sagas, but just the kind of mindless entertainment she needed at the moment. Her own plight seemed minute when compared to the larger than life happenings on the screen and she thought herself thoroughly engrossed in the movie, until she awoke some time later and found she'd slept through most of it.

The young man beside her had also fallen asleep,

and she shook him awake after the captain announced their approach to Heathrow. "Tell me," she said to him, "are you familiar with the airport?"

He nodded. "Pretty familiar. I've been there a few times."

"Will I be able to change clothes before going through passport control?"

"No, I don't believe so."

"Then I'm going to have to change now. Except I'm afraid there's going to be trouble if the flight attendants see me suddenly transformed from a boy to a woman."

"Just take off your hat and put on some lipstick when we get off the plane."

"I have a wig in my bag."

"Leave it for later. They might be watching the airport, you know."

"But my passport picture has me as a blonde."

"So you changed your hair color. Women are known to do such things."

To her seat partner's amazement, Julie reached up under her shirt and removed the wrapping that was holding her in. When she'd retrieved all of it, she shoved it into her bag beneath the seat as she studiously avoided his eyes. Her chest had been getting more attention lately than she could handle.

Immediately after getting off the plane, she took off her baseball shirt to reveal a T-shirt beneath and quickly put on some lipstick.

"That's better," her companion said, "now take off the hat."

Julie did, putting it and the shirt into her bag. "Do I look strange?" she asked him.

"A little, but people are used to crazy Americans."

The man at Passport Control looked from her to her picture several times, then seemed satisfied it was merely a change of hair color.

"Will you be in Great Britain long?" he asked her.

"Just a few days."

"Business or pleasure?"

"Business."

"And your business?"

She sighed, wishing she'd said pleasure. "I'm an economist, I'm here for a conference."

They seemed to be magic words because his formally dour expression turned to a smile. "Good. We can use all the help with our economy that we can get. Good luck, miss."

I never knew I had such a talent for lying, Julie thought to herself as she headed for the ladies' room. Once inside she changed into her dress and sandals, then put her new blond wig on her head. The length was ludicrous. She looked like the stereotype of a Country/Western singer and was afraid she was going to find it an impossibility to blend into the crowd. Trust her little brother to come up with such a tacky wig.

But it was thanks to that same little brother that she was here at all. Thinking it might have sentimental value for him, she stuffed Wally's baseball suit back into his bag to return to him.

Mustafa was waiting for her outside the door. It annoyed her that he recognized her so readily.

"How'd you know it was me?"

He grinned. "You're carrying the same bag. Don't worry, no one else will recognize you. And may I say, the change is quite an improvement. I think you are even better looking than your sister."

She didn't acknowledge the compliment, certain it was due in large part to her flowing mane.

"How do I get to London from here?" she asked him.

"The airline has a bus at the airport that will take us to Victoria Station, which is how I'm traveling. Come along, we'll go together."

"Look, I really don't want your help."

"Then I promise I won't help you; we'll just travel together, all right?"

As it turned out, she was glad she'd taken him up on the offer. The bus was filled largely with men, men who seemed attracted to blondes with long hair. The wig was tight and heavy and by the time they arrived she had a headache and longed to take it off. Since it swung around and covered most of her face, however, she decided she better go with it. It was probably a better disguise than most.

Victoria Station was bedlam, filled with tourists, most of them young. There were kids encamped on every bench and rows of them along the walls, sleeping on the floor. If she'd still been in her baseball suit she would've considered joining them as she'd have blended in perfectly. As it was, though, she wanted to look at least halfway respectable when she showed up at the TV studio.

"What are you going to do now?" Mustafa asked her.

Julie spied a pub on the premises. "I'm going to get a drink."

"They're not serving at this hour.'

"Then I'm going to get some sleep."

Mustafa took her arm. "Why don't you come with me. My friends would be honored to supply you with a bed. No drinks, though; they're religious."

She leaned over and kissed him on the cheek. "Thanks for the offer, Mustafa, but I want to do this alone. I'll be all right—honest."

He spread his arms. "Where will you sleep? There's not an empty space anywhere."

She grinned at him. "Just watch." She headed in the direction of one of the benches where she saw some young men talking, using up more room than they needed.

"You guys American?" she asked them, tossing her blond hair back as she spoke.

"Yes, you want to join us?" Already they were making room for her.

"Don't mind if I do," she told them, then slid down in the seat, using her bag as a pillow, and promptly fell asleep.

Chapter Twelve

"Who?"

"Harry Blake. He works there."

"No Harry Blake here, miss. Sorry."

Julie turned from the call box, shoulders sagging in dejection, and almost bumped into Mustafa, who was handing her a container of coffee.

"You're still here?" she asked, warming her hands on the sides of the cardboard container. The station was cool and damp and judging from the condition of the people who'd been entering, it was raining outside.

"I stayed the night in case you might need me."

It would seem she'd got this far only to be defeated in the end. "I was to give the film to a friend of Emery's at the BBC, but there's no one by that name in their employ."

"Could you have got the name wrong?" he suggested gently.

She shook her head. "I don't see how. Harry Blake is a fairly simple name."

"You won't give up, will you?"

She looked at his tired face. He looked as though he'd been standing all night with no sleep at all. He seemed much too young to be involved, to be carrying the burdens of his people on his narrow shoulders. She straightened up, took a drink of the tepid coffee, and managed a smile.

"No, I won't give up, Mustafa. I guess I could go over to the BBC and see if someone in their news department would speak to me."

He suddenly looked less tired. "I will go with you."

"You don't need to; you look like you could use some sleep."

"There will be time enough for sleep later. Right now I think you might need my help." He was shrugging out of his cotton windbreaker and handing it to her. "Here, wear this; you'll be too cold in that thin dress."

She saw that his shirt beneath the jacket was long sleeved and gratefully accepted his offer. She obviously hadn't been thinking when she'd chosen a thin, sleeveless dress to bring along. She should have remembered that August in England was notorious for its cold.

"We'll get a taxi to the BBC, but first I think we should have some breakfast," said Mustafa, taking charge.

Julie allowed herself to be led out of Victoria Station and down several crowded streets to where Mustafa stopped at a café and opened the door for her.

The inside of the café smelled of wet wool and rubber boots with an overlay of spices. The counter was three deep with people trying to get their morning tea. Mustafa pointed her toward an empty table and Julie was barely seated before a steaming mug of tea was set in front of her.

She drank it halfway down and it worked to revive her somewhat, but her head was still aching and with one, swift gesture she took the blonde wig from her head and stowed it away in her zippered bag. Several heads turned at the sight of the blonde being suddenly transformed into a brunette and the beginning of a smile appeared on Mustafa's serious young face.

She ran her fingers through her hair feeling relief as soon as the pressure of the tight wig was gone. She smiled at Mustafa. "Now I feel myself again."

"I don't think you need a disguise anymore. I kept a close watch at the station all night and didn't see anyone recognizable as a Mossad agent."

She didn't point out that if they were any good they wouldn't be recognizable. It was strange, but somehow she felt safer in London than she had in New York. And for some unaccountable reason she trusted Mustafa. He wasn't pushing her to do anything; he was just there in case she should need him.

The Indian waiter took their order and returned in a few minutes with eggs and sausages, both smelling strangely of curry powder. She looked around at the other customers and saw that they all looked foreign, or at least not English. It was rather like being in New York in that respect.

Mustafa paid the bill as they didn't take credit cards and Julie hadn't changed any money. In order to save time, she allowed him to pay for the taxi also, reimbursing him in American dollars.

The cab was enormous and she settled back in its cavernous interior and wondered what would happen at the BBC. She was aware she wasn't going to present a prepossessing picture to the people in charge there. She should have dressed either more business-like or more guerillalike, but instead would look like something dragged in off the street. Her name should open a few doors, though; her father was known worldwide.

Julie opened her bag and took out a compact, scrutinizing her reflection in the small mirror. Her hair was looking better; the rain had made it fluff out and soft curls were beginning to form around her face. Soft greenish curls, she noted with wry amusement. She applied lipstick, then dusted her face with powder. She must have got some color at the beach because her cheeks were flushed and she looked decidedly healthy despite her lack of sleep. She found herself hoping that Noah had got a bad burn and was even now suffering the effects.

The BBC's receptionist used every means available to dissuade Julie, ignoring her at first, then making her wait for almost an hour. But Julie was insistent and at last, with a show of churlishness, the woman condescended to call one of the men in the news department.

"I don't rightly know who she is, sir," Julie heard her say, and then called out, "Tell him I'm John Domino's daughter."

The woman gave her an outraged look, but repeated the information, then turned to Julie, and with more courtesy than she had previously shown, informed her that Mr. Fellows would see her briefly.

Moments later a tall, sandy-haired man appeared and held out his hand to Julie. "Ian Fellows. And I understand you're John Domino's daughter."

Julie stood and introduced herself and Mustafa. They followed Ian Fellows back to his small office were he ordered tea for them all. "Now tell me what this is all about."

"First of all, Mr. Fellows, I don't want to mislead you into thinking this has anything to do with my father. In fact, I'm afraid he'd disapprove of what I'm doing."

"Yes, well, that's the case with fathers, isn't it?" he joked, putting her at her ease.

"I came here on my sister's behalf, not his. She told me to see Harry Blake of the BBC, but when I called..." She stopped speaking when she saw what effect her words were having on him. For an already pale person, he had grown considerably whiter in a very short space of time.

"Did you say Harry Blake?" He almost whispered the words.

"Why, yes, but the receptionist had never heard of him."

Mr. Fellows's color was gradually returning. "Harry Blake isn't a person, Miss Domino. It's more of a—well, you might call it a password or even a signal, if you see what I mean."

"I'm afraid I don't."

"I'm afraid I'm not able to explain it any better at

this time. Perhaps it would be best if you were to tell me what you want.''

Julie looked over at Mustafa who was nodding his head. ''Tell him the whole story, Julie; that way he'll understand.''

Forty minutes and three cups of tea later, Julie's story wound down and she saw that Ian Fellows was looking at her with a new degree of respect.

''And you say you have the film with you?''

Julie reached into her bag and brought it out, placing it in his outstretched hand. She was almost hesitant to let it go at this point after guarding it for so long.

''Perhaps we should take a look at it,'' he suggested.

''I'd like that,'' said Julie. ''I've never seen it.''

More tea was ordered before he took them to a projection room where a cameraman was all set to go. For the next few minutes Julie sat in the dark room and watched the flickering images on the screen, wondering what all the fuss was about. It was shot from such a distance she couldn't tell what the men looked like except that they were wearing the distinctive PLO headdresses.

When she mentioned this, Mr. Fellows said, ''True enough, but we can get enlargements made for identification purposes. All in all, your sister got herself an exceptional bit of footage here. I think it's possible my bosses will be very eager to show this. I'll have to make a few phone calls, speak to a few people, but I think we could tentatively schedule this for the evening news. With some corroboration, of course.''

"What kind of corroboration?" Julie asked him.

"Your sister would be the best. But if we can't get her, we'll use that old catchword 'alleged,' when we show it."

He led them back to his office. "Where will you be in case I need to reach you?" he asked Julie.

"Couldn't I stick around here?"

"That's not really necessary, you know. You can rest assured it's in good hands. I'll tell you what, though; you can come back tonight for the actual broadcast, if you'd like. Both of you, of course."

Julie thought of a warm bath, a bed, perhaps a change of clothes. "Could you recommend a hotel?"

"I have just the thing for you," he told her. "We maintain a suite at the Inter-Continental for BBC guests; I think you'd qualify. I'll give them a call so they'll be expecting you."

He offered them one final cup of tea before they left, but Julie declined, afraid she'd float away if she imbibed any more.

At the entrance to the building she parted company with Mustafa, after promising to meet him in front of the building a few minutes before seven.

Too keyed up to sleep, Julie had a taxi driver drop her off at Oxford Street where she walked until she came to Giorgio Armani's. Once inside she found a lightweight wool suit that was perfect for London in August and New York throughout the winter months.

Down the street at Brown's she found shoes and a silky shirt to wear with her suit, and further on at Molton Brown she went inside and turned herself over to a hairdresser, saying only that she wanted her hair permanently dark. An hour later she emerged with her hair a lustrous shade of mahogany that she hoped she'd be able to duplicate in New York.

She checked in at the Inter-Continental and allowed the bellboy to carry her packages up to the suite for her. The rooms were elegantly furnished and modern with a view from the window of Hyde Park. She put her new purchases away, then ran water in the oversized tub for a bath.

Julie undressed in front of a mirror and noticed that she'd got quite a bit of color at the beach. Which reminded her of Noah, unfortunately, a subject she'd sooner forget. She stepped into the tub and slipped her hand into the bath mit provided, wondering if she'd ever see him again. Wondering if she even wanted to see him again.

It wasn't as though there'd been any future in it to begin with. Still she was sorry that her memories of him were now tainted by that final scene on the boardwalk. She played it over again in her mind. She could've sworn he'd had some real feelings for her; was it possible he was so consummate an actor? What bothered her the most was that she'd never know. It was very much like playing a small scene in a movie without knowing what the rest of the film was about.

But then there was never any way of knowing what another person felt; there never had been. Ninety-nine percent of a person's thoughts, loves, hates, fears were impossible to communicate. Everyone in the world was locked inside himself from the day of birth to the day of death making true communication between man and woman impossible except by touch.

Julie was beginning to feel the effects of lack of sleep as she toweled herself dry, and with nothing else to do, decided upon a nap. She got into Wally's baseball suit, closed the curtains across the windows and slipped beneath the covers of one of the beds.

She was looking forward to seeing the broadcast that night, but after that she was afraid she'd be in for a letdown. The last few days had been so filled with adventure, boarding airplanes becoming as natural to her as taking a subway, that the idea of returning to her small apartment and resuming her quiet life no longer held great appeal.

Well, there was no reason she couldn't stay on in London for a few days and play at being a tourist. She had nothing to do until school started. She could see some plays, do some shopping and just generally take in the sights. Perhaps she would stop by the London School of Economics and look into the possibility of teaching there the following year. Everyone else in her family seemed to be seeing the world, why shouldn't she?

The more she thought about it the more she liked the idea. And if LSE wasn't interested, there was always Italy. She was sure she could get a job there in one of the universities. She knew the language and the weather there was certainly preferable to either London or New York. It was time she got out of her safe, familiar environment and saw something more of the world. It would please her family, too; and speaking of her family...

She reached for the phone beside the bed and placed a call to New York.

Her father's voice came over the wires sounding as close as the next room. "Hello, Julie, is that you?"

"Yes, Dad, I'm in London."

"Good, then you made it."

"I guess you've talked to Emery."

"She told us you were off to the BBC. Everything go all right?"

She was hesitating over what to tell him, when she added, "I think you did the right thing, Julie."

So Emery had managed to convince him where she had failed. "I'm glad you feel that way, Dad. I was afraid you'd be upset."

"No, I've always said you had a good head on your shoulders; you made the right decision. By the way, I have some friends at the BBC if you have any problems."

"No problems. They're showing the film tonight."

"Well, good show, and all that, as the British say. We'll be seeing you sometime tomorrow then?"

"I may stay on for a few days."

"You deserve the vacation, honey; enjoy yourself."

"I will, Dad, and thanks," she said before hanging up the phone.

Emery must have been her usual persuasive self to have convinced her father that what she was doing was right. But then Emery had always been his favorite, able to talk him into just about anything. Just as her mother had always favored Wally. Which was all right with her as she'd got along the best with all of them.

Julie slept for several hours, awakening suddenly to a darkened room with no recollection of where she was. She lay in the dark for a moment until the events of the last few hours returned to her, then got up and opened the curtains. She saw she had some time before leaving for the studio and called room service to have tea sent up.

The waiter brought a silver teapot of Georgian design along with a plate of small sandwiches. He placed it on a table in front of a fireplace and only glanced briefly at Julie's baseball suit. He probably thought her an eccentric American.

She decided tea was a very civilized custom and finished off all the sandwiches and the entire pot. She was feeling well rested and entirely revived by the time she started to dress.

She applied makeup carefully before putting on her new clothes, and when she had finished she was pleased with the results. She wished Noah could see her now looking elegant yet businesslike and totally different from the way he'd seen her before. For the first time she seemed to fit into the luxury surroundings.

She took a taxi to the BBC, and waiting for her outside was Mustafa, looking pretty elegant himself in suit and tie. They went up in the lift together like old friends, both of them excited about what was about to transpire.

Ian came out to the reception area immediately, his eyes alight. "I have a surprise for you," he said to her.

"I hope the film's going to be shown."

"Oh, it is, it is," he assured her, shepherding them both back to his office. "But I think the surprise will be the icing on the cake. I know it was for us."

And there, seated in Ian's office and looking like the consummate guerrilla, the epitome of revolutionary fashion in battle fatigues by Balenciaga, was Emery.

She leaped to her feet at their entrance, with a half-embrace and a clap on the back for Julie and a comrade's handshake for an overawed Mustafa. It would seem that her sister had struck a pose as the latest heroine of the PLO and found it mesmerizing.

"Your sister flew over here in order to narrate the film for us tonight," Ian was saying.

"How'd you get out of there?" Julie asked her, her last view of Emery having been when she'd run into the restroom at the beach.

"It's a long story, sweetie, I'll tell you all about it later."

"Just tell me why you—" Julie began.

Emery gave her a quelling look. "Later, darling—please!"

As usual, her sister was taking control.

Ian took them to the news studio where Julie and Mustafa were seated in the control booth and Emery took her place beside Ian at a table in front of the cameras. Julie was sitting there in nervous anticipation when just minutes before the telecast was to begin, she saw a flustered young man run into the studio and hand a piece of paper to Ian.

Ian's face seemed to drop as he read it, then wordlessly he handed it to Emery. Emery was clearly flustered, her mouth moving and her hands waving around, and Julie wished she could hear what was going on in the studio.

She found out soon enough when the telecast began. In measured tones, Ian announced that an Israeli spokesman had just announced from the floor of the Knesset that the hijacking of just days before had been perpetrated by a group of West Bank youths in protest over the dismantling of their village.

All that for nothing, Julie was thinking, feeling deflated. She glanced next to her to see Mustafa's reaction, but he seemed to be taking it better than her.

"Don't worry," he said to her in a low voice, patting her hand. "It's all right. We forced them to admit it, don't you see?"

As an adjunct to the news bulletin, Ian then announced that the BBC had the only existing film of the hijacking and that with him in the studio was the American photojournalist who had taken the film.

The hijacking appeared on the TV monitors while Emery's voice told the viewing audience the circumstances that had made it possible for her to get the film. Julie could see that Emery became larger than life in front of the camera as though she took sustenance in imagining that she occupied space in other people's lives, the lives of strangers. Perhaps even the lives of countries.

No mention was made of the difficulties in getting the film from Athens to Beirut to New York and then to London, however, and Julie had a feeling the full story would never be told.

Julie felt as if she'd been betrayed somehow. She could understand the Israelis thinking the information would sound better coming from them, but she couldn't help being sorry the film hadn't come as a surprise to the world. It made all she'd gone through the past few days seem ludicrous; especially the part where Noah was concerned.

Afterwards, in Ian's office, he opened a bottle of champagne and filled glasses for them. He proposed a toast to the BBC's scoop, and Julie listlessly lifted her glass with the others.

"It was still worth it, Julie, believe me," said Emery, as though reading her thoughts.

"Truly it was," Mustafa echoed her.

But then neither of them knew how involved she'd actually been. She didn't think it was even worth having her apartment torn apart, let alone her emotions. For a five-minute news story that would be forgotten by tomorrow her life had been in total upheaval for the past few days, and she didn't think it was going to be so easy to put back together again.

Ian seemed to understand her feelings a little. "Well, at least you got to London," he told her.

"Yes, and I want to thank you for the use of the suite. It's lovely there. In fact, I'm thinking of staying on for a few days."

"Please feel free to stay on there if you do. We don't need it for at least a week. And if you want tickets to any of the shows, you need only ask."

"Maybe I'll stay on with you," Emery said to her. "I can't remember when I last had a vacation."

Julie wasn't overjoyed at the prospect. She'd had in mind a quiet vacation and quiet was an unknown to her sister.

Julie and Emery took leave of Mustafa outside the building, where the young man practically swore his allegiance to her sister before he and Julie quietly embraced and said their good-byes. Then Emery was hailing a taxi and they were soon driving back to the Inter-Continental.

"Do you want to get dinner?" Julie asked Emery once they were in the lobby of the hotel.

Emery gave her an enigmatic look. "Later, darling; first I'd like to go upstairs for a bit."

Emery was silent in the lift and silent as they walked together down the carpeted hallway to the door of her suite. Julie inserted the key in the door and was surprised to see lights on inside. She could clearly remember turning them off when she left.

A few feet into the suite she saw them. Noah was seated in a chair, a cigarette in his hand. And leaning casually against the fireplace was Yotav, looking cosmopolitan in a double-breasted blue blazer with a voluminous foulard tucked around his throat.

She turned to see Emery's reaction, but her sister was already flying across the room and straight into Yotav's waiting arms.

Julie just stood there in shocked silence as all knowns dissolved and rearranged themselves into unknowns. "I think I must be losing my mind," she murmured, and turned to go back out the door.

Chapter Thirteen

"Julie!"

It was Noah calling her back. She ignored him and stepped out into the hallway. Her thoughts were in turmoil and she couldn't yet begin to fathom why her sister and her sister's reputed archenemy were now boisterously embracing a few scant feet behind her. And some people found economics difficult to understand!

She was halfway down the hall on her way to the elevators when Noah ran up behind her and grabbed her unceremoniously by the arm. "Come back in the room, darling—we have to talk."

She questioned the "darling" with the almost imperceptible movement of one eyebrow before firmly disengaging her arm from his hand and continuing on down the hall.

"Look, there's a lot you don't understand," he persisted.

No kidding. She didn't understand any of it, and furthermore she wasn't sure she wanted to. She reached the bank of elevators and pressed the button.

"I know it must look strange to you to see me and Yotav together, to say nothing of your sister."

It looked more than strange; it looked ominous. "Forget it, Colonel Majors. You might have got to my sister, but you're not getting to me." Which would have been a good exit line if the elevators had seen fit to cooperate at that moment. Instead, she was left standing there, studiously ignoring him, when Emery came out of the suite and headed in their direction.

"Sweetie, what's gotten into you? Come on back. We're ordering up drinks from room service and I think we need to have ourselves a cozy chat."

Emery was close enough now for Julie to see the expression on her face, and she didn't like what she saw. Her sister had the same smug, self-satisfied look she'd had when she'd stolen Mark Collier away from her back in their high school days. Emery was at her happiest when everything was going Emery's way.

"I'll leave you three to your celebration party," Julie said with dignity. "I'm going to dinner. And Emery, I'd appreciate it if all of you were gone by the time I return."

"Julie, what's the matter with you?" said Emery, looking to Noah for support in the kind of helpless female way she could summon up when necessary. Only to Julie there was something incongruous about a woman dressed like an urban guerrilla pretending to be helpless. "Tell her to come back, Noah," she pleaded, all but batting her eyes at Teddy Bear.

Noah turned his attention to Emery. "I believe your sister has a mind of her own."

Emery dropped the helpless act and appealed directly to Julie. "What's the matter with you? You've been absolutely marvelous up to now; we're all very proud of you."

"I'm not very proud of me," Julie told her. "What are you, Emery, CIA? Mossad? Or do you just freelance?"

Emery looked to Noah, who merely said, "Come on, Julie; this isn't something we can discuss in the hall."

"Why not? Is the hallway of the Inter-Continental bugged?"

The elevator finally arrived and Julie stepped inside. Noah put his hand on the door to stop it from closing.

"Oh, let her go," said Emery. "If she wants to go off and sulk like a child, I'm not going to stop her." She turned to go back to the suite and after hesitating for a moment, Noah got into the elevator with Julie.

Julie pressed the button for the lobby and retreated into the far corner of the lift.

"There's no need for you to cower over there; I'm not going to attack you in the elevator."

"Go back with your friends, Noah; we have nothing to say to each other."

"I had a feeling your sister was wrong. She seemed to think you'd be amused by the whole thing."

"Oh, but I am. I always find being used vastly amusing."

"Julie—"

"Knock off the entreaties, Noah—they're not going to work. I'm going to go out and get myself some dinner, then come back here and get some sleep—alone—and after that I'm going home and try to forget any of this ever happened."

"Don't you even want to hear about it?"

"No." The elevator stopped and she got out, heading for the restaurant she'd seen off the lobby.

Ordinarily she'd consider La Soufflé's prices beyond her means, but tonight she didn't care. Her American Express card would take care of the immediate problem, and she'd worry later about all the charges she'd been running up of late. In fact maybe, just maybe, she'd send Emery a bill. It was about time her sister paid for the consequences of her actions.

The maitre d', assuming they were together, led them both to a quiet table off to one side and Julie didn't know how to get rid of Noah without embarrassment. And while she was tempted to make a scene for the first time in her life, dignity won out, and she allowed herself to be seated across from him. But if he was stupid enough to think they were going to enjoy a pleasant meal together, he was sorely mistaken. She was finding his company just slightly preferable to her sister's at the moment.

The disparity between the romantic setting, complete with candlelight, and the way she was feeling about Noah, wasn't lost on her. Just twenty-four hours earlier she would have loved to dine with him in just such a setting. Now she thought his presence might easily precipitate an ulcer.

She waited in silence until the waiter appeared. Rather than simplify things by handing them menus, he recited it to them in much the same way God must have sounded when he handed down the ten commandments. Rather like her father, she mused.

Julie ordered a cheese soufflé, and in answer to the waiter's question as to what kind of cheese, she told him she didn't care. When Noah told him he'd take the same, and added a bottle of red wine to the order, specifying that he didn't care what kind, just make it fast, the irate waiter retreated.

"You're looking very well. Quite sophisticated in that suit," Noah said appreciatively.

Julie ignored the ill-timed compliment, noting at the same time that Noah looked his usual disheveled self. It did occur to her that she'd eaten with him far more often than they'd made love. Which was just as well, she supposed, looking over the other diners in an effort to ignore him.

Noah wasn't taking well to being ignored. "You know what? I got a sunburn, how about you?"

It was at times like this Julie wished she smoked. It would give her something to do besides looking everywhere but at the man across from her, who she could see out of the corner of her eyes was looking only at her. And talking about sunburn, as if that had any importance at all.

"That touch—using Wally at your window—that was clever, Julie."

"Not clever enough," she muttered under her breath.

"That's only because I know you so well. I recognized your walk."

Her self-imposed silence came to a sudden end.

"My walk? What do you mean my walk? I was walking like a boy."

"Ah, got your attention at last, did I? It wasn't a boy's walk, Julie. It was you trying to walk like a boy. There's a difference, you know. Anyway, it didn't matter; we knew where you were going."

"Don't you occasionally have trouble living with yourself, Noah?"

"It does get lonely, living alone."

"That's not what I'm talking about. Doesn't it bother you at all to use women like that?"

"It's just part of the job. Anyway, using you wasn't my idea; your sister came up with that one."

"It was Emery's idea that you seduce me?"

"I didn't seduce you; it was mutual."

"I hardly consider it mutual when you were doing it as part of your job."

He grinned at her. "Oh, is that what's bothering you? It was never part of the job, Julie. You would have done what we wanted with or without the sex."

The wine arrived, was decanted and their glasses filled. Julie took a long swallow and hoped the food would arrive before her anger would become such she'd feel it incumbent upon her to get up and leave. And she was fast approaching that point.

"It does bother me, Noah. All of it bothers me. When was it Yotav got to her, was it in Beirut?"

"What're you talking about?"

"I'm asking when it was my sister got so chummy with Yotav. Was it when he took her into custody the first time?"

"You've got it wrong, Julie. Did you think she

suddenly turned traitor, so to speak, at some point?''

''Didn't she?''

''No way—your sister was in on it from the start.''

''The start? You mean she contacted you when she happened to get the hijacking on film?''

''Before that.''

''But how could it have been before that? She wouldn't have known about the hijacking before that. Or would she?''

He nodded. ''Mossad set up the hijacking.''

Her mind was becoming mass confusion with none of the facts coalescing in any way that made sense to her. ''Why would they do that?''

''In order for your sister to make contact with the PLO. Which she did.''

''Whom does she work for, Noah?'' Quietly, with restrained fury.

''I think Emery should be the one to answer that question.''

''I'm asking you.'' She stopped speaking while the soufflés were placed in front of them. ''And if I don't get an answer, I'm going to be very tempted to dump that soufflé in your lap!''

''She's been with the CIA for years, Julie; we recruited her when she was still in college. She had this natural facility for languages that would have been wasted if she'd just taught school.''

Which showed her how much he valued her own profession. ''And the filmmaking? Whose idea was that?''

''She was fooling around with it anyway, taking a

few courses. And you have to admit it's a great cover."

"Plus it put her quite naturally in all the world's hot spots, right?"

He smiled. "Right! She's been one of our most successful operatives. And it doesn't hurt that she's a good-looking, sexy woman, either."

She vowed he'd pay for that remark. "And I always admired what she was doing. I thought she had convictions, the kind I lacked."

"And she does. She's worth admiring, Julie."

She gave him a look of scorn. "I'm afraid I find nothing admirable in being a spy, Noah."

He had the good sense to keep quiet at that remark.

"In fact I find the whole business despicable."

Noah took a sudden interest in his soufflé, going so far as to loudly smack his lips in pleasure.

Her generalized anger was becoming more specific, but instead of zeroing in on the real source, she made a sudden turn to the right and focussed it on Emery. Her darling sister, without whom she'd have remained blissfully ignorant of all such devious machinations.

"I cannot tell you how appalled, how utterly disgusted I am at finding my sister employed by the CIA."

Noah's expression was benign. "That's putting it a bit strong, I'd say."

"Would you?" Scathingly. "I'd say words don't adequately express just how strongly I feel."

"Come on, Julie—give her a break. After all, she's only following in your father's footsteps."

"Oh, no—don't tell me Daddy..." Her voice, sounding very young, faltered.

"For heaven's sake, Julie, you make it sound criminal."

"I think it's worse than criminal!"

He stopped eating and reached across the table to take hold of her hand, almost crushing it as he spoke. "Now you listen to me, Julie: Since when is keeping your country safe a criminal act? Will you tell me that?"

"Everyone knows the CIA—"

"Don't you tell me what everyone knows—I've been there. Who are you to talk, anyway, sitting on that NYU campus in your ivory tower. When have you ever confronted the realities of life? Theories, that's all you know. You sit there spouting economic principles while your sister, and others like her, are out there making it possible for you to continue doing just that. As her father did before her." He let go of her hand and sat back in his chair. "Now why don't you admit what's really bothering you? And don't pretend that it's your sister or the CIA or any other claptrap you can conveniently dig up. It's you and me that has you all riled up, admit it."

"That's partly true, Noah, but it isn't all of the truth. There was also a very nice young man I flew over with, who thought the truth was important and who now thinks of my sister as some kind of heroine. This touched more than just us, Noah."

He spoke gently. "He was one of us, Julie."

She felt tears spring to her eyes at the final disillusionment. "But he couldn't be. He told me about growing up in a camp, it was all so real. I just can't believe that, Noah.''

"Oh, that was true enough, his background. But once he got to college in the States and tasted the good life, well, he was open to recruitment."

"So you even had to poison *his* life."

"It was his choice, Julie; we didn't force him."

She pushed the plate with the uneaten soufflé away from her and stood up. "I've heard enough for tonight, Noah; I don't think I can take anymore."

"Sit back down in that chair!"

Too defeated to argue, she did as he said. She had a feeling it was almost over now. He'd make a few more excuses for behavior that was innately inexcusable, no doubt rationalize his more personal conduct towards her, all in an attempt to put the final wraps on the case. And never knowing, or even caring, how he'd touched her life.

"I want to talk about us, Julie."

"Us? There is no 'us.' There never was."

"Will you wipe your eyes and quit trying to turn this into some tragedy? There most definitely was an 'us,' Julie, and what's more, there still is."

Julie sighed and managed to look bored. She'd be damned if she'd let him get to her again. "Just say what you have to say, Noah."

"I'm in love with you, Julie."

Her eyes widened slightly, but otherwise she didn't betray the fact that what he said meant anything to her.

"Well? Can't you say anything? I just told you I loved you."

She shrugged. "So what?"

"So what? Is that all you can say? This happens to be the first time I've said those words to a woman since I was married, and all you can say is so what?" Flustered, now, and a little angry.

"Is that supposed to excuse what happened?"

"No, no it's not. I don't need to excuse what happened. I have no regrets, and neither should you. What I'm trying to find out, and not succeeding at too well, is how you feel about me."

"How I feel about you isn't important."

"To me it is! Damn it, Julie, how can you just sit there and stare at me like I was some total stranger?"

"Why not? I never really knew you."

Noah looked as though he'd like to leap the distance across the table and wring her neck. "You can really be exasperating. If I live to be a million, I don't think I'll ever understand women."

"Then why try?"

Noah seemed to slump in his seat. "Look, Julie, can you honestly say you don't feel anything towards me?"

"No, that wouldn't be true. At the moment I feel a great deal of anger towards you, and a certain lingering revulsion."

"Not even any physical attraction?"

She shook her head. "Not at the moment, no."

He spread his arms in a supplicating gesture. "Then there's nothing more I can say, I guess."

She started to get up but was stopped by his words. "Tell me something, Julie. Are you equally as revolted by your father?"

"He's always been the most important man in my life, Noah. I can't yet believe what you've told me about him."

"And Emery? Are you revolted by her?"

She gave a mirthless laugh. "No more so by this than by other things she's done. Although to deliberately involve me in it . . ."

"It could just as easily have been your brother."

"What do you mean?"

"Just that we weren't sure which of you would be sent over to find your sister."

"At least you wouldn't have become personally involved with Wally. At least I don't think so."

"Julie, if you have any doubts whatsoever about that—"

She chuckled. "No. I have no doubts."

As though encouraged by her humor, he poured them each more wine. "How about giving me another chance, Julie? We could go upstairs and throw out Emery and Yotav. I know, if I could just get you alone . . ."

Julie smiled at the remembrance that she had once again packed sans diaphragm. "I'm afraid not, Noah."

"Are you saying you really don't have any feelings for me?"

"I'll get over it."

"Hell, Julie—I don't want you to get over it!"

"Well, you don't always get what you want, Noah!"

"Look, will you at least eat your dinner? Let's forget everything else and just have a good meal together."

Julie looked down at the cold soufflé huddled on her plate as though to warm itself. He was getting to her again and she didn't like it. Any more time spent with him and she was afraid her self-control was going to break down and she'd end up once more in his arms, and that was a sure way to disaster. Having a brief affair with a spy was one thing; having a love affair with him was a danger to her way of life.

"Tell me something, Noah; were you attracted to Emery?"

"Hell no!"

"Then why me? Everyone else takes us for one another."

"You're nothing like your sister."

"But I look like her."

"That doesn't mean anything; you're totally different. Her type never did appeal to me."

Julie couldn't stop the smile from spreading across her face. Since seeing them all together in the hotel suite she'd been wondering if Noah and Emery had ever been together. She'd been on the receiving line of Emery's leftovers before and now, as then, she couldn't stomach the idea.

"Listen, Julie, you want to go to the beach?"

"The beach?"

"Yeah, you like the beach, right?"

"Noah, it's not only night, it's freezing here."

"I'm not talking about England. Come back to Greece with me. I'll take you to Mykonos; I hear it has great beaches."

"Thanks for the offer, but no."

"You have anything better to do? Come on, let's

have a little vacation together, see if we can't work things out.''

The idea had appeal. More appeal than staying on in London, or even returning to New York. But just as a matter of personal survival, she thought she'd forget Noah faster and easier if she never saw him again after tonight when a residue of anger towards him still remained. Once in Greece with him, she might never want to return home.

"I don't think it's a very good idea, Noah."

She signaled for the waiter and asked for the check while Noah sat in silence. She insisted on paying the bill, not wanting to owe him anything, then he walked with her to the elevators.

"Good-bye, Noah," she said, holding out her hand.

He ignored it. "I think you're making a mistake," he said.

"It won't be the first time."

"Look, Julie, I'm going to be staying at the embassy tonight. Call me in the morning if you change your mind, okay?"

Her last view of him when the doors to the elevator closed was of a very sad, dejected-looking teddy bear of a man. And how deceiving that appearance was, she mused as the lift carried her up to her floor. Teddy bears might be lovable; spies weren't!

She knocked on the door to her suite before using her key to let herself in. What she found wasn't Emery and Yotav in a compromising position, though, unless you could call eating compromising. It seemed they had called room service, and were both busily consuming steak dinners that looked appealing to Julie, who had suddenly regained her appetite.

"Where's Noah?" Yotav asked her.

She ignored him and instead spoke to her sister. "I thought I told you to be out of here when I returned."

"Oh, Julie, you're not still mad, are you?"

Julie took off her suit jacket and hung it up, then sat down on the loveseat near where they were seated. "I think I have every reason to be, Emery. Was it really necessary for you to lie to me? Couldn't you have just explained the situation to me and asked for my help?"

Emery gave her a skeptical look. "And would you have helped?"

"Probably not, but that's my prerogative, isn't it?"

Yotav was looking between the two of them, and finally asked Emery, "Would you rather I left?"

"No," said Emery.

"Yes," said Julie.

He put down his fork, placed his linen napkin on the table, and stood up. "I for one wish to thank you," he said, bowing in Julie's direction. "You have done my country a great service and we are grateful."

Julie ignored him and soon she heard the door to the suite close behind him. She moved to take the seat across from Emery, helping herself to Yotav's uneaten roll. She ate it slowly, noting that her sister was becoming unnerved by her silence.

"I think there's something I ought to tell you," Emery finally said.

"Noah already told me."

Emery tried her charming smile. "Well, then you understand."

"I understand you've been playing at being a spy."

"I'd hardly call it playing, Julie."

"It's your life, Emery; what I don't appreciate is your involving me in it. I don't recall choosing to be a spy."

Emery's eyes took on a gleam. "Don't give me that school teacher tone of voice of yours. Admit it, you enjoyed every minute of it."

"Oh, yes, I always enjoy having my life turned upside down, going without sleep, visiting battle zones. It was a lark!"

Emery chuckled. "What's more, you were marvelous at it. Yotav thinks you have a natural talent, and I agree."

"Whatever you're leading up to, Emery—forget it!"

"But we'd make a marvelous team. Can't you see it? The two of us look so much alike, we could get away with anything."

"Is this a recruitment speech I'm hearing?"

"Call it what you like. I've been authorized to approach you."

Julie began to cut up what remained of Yotav's steak. The baked potato, unfortunately, had already been demolished. "Was this Noah's idea?"

"No, but I'm sure he'd concur. I know he seems to think you're pretty special."

Julie refilled Yotav's teacup and added lemon and sugar. "The answer, Emery, is no."

In a devious gesture, Emery moved her baked potato, which was still intact, over onto what had now become Julie's plate. "Be honest, Julie, wasn't it more fun than teaching school?"

"I happen to like teaching school." She put a dollop of butter on the baked potato and took a bite.

"Really, Julie, sometimes I despair of you. Preferring that dreary existence of yours to living a life of adventure out in the real world. Your intelligence is much too good to be wasted on such mundane matters as economics."

Julie stopped eating long enough to say, "At least I sleep with a clear conscience at night."

"And you think I don't?" Emery laughed. "I honestly don't know how our illustrious parents ever spawned someone like you."

"Speaking of which, Noah told me Dad was also involved."

Emery was shaking her head. "Not anymore. He did the odd job for them when he was a foreign correspondent, but that's normal operating procedure. He was never really on the payroll."

"I'm relieved to hear it."

Emery cocked her head to one side. "He's always been your hero, hasn't he? And you've probably measured every man you've ever met by him, I imagine."

That was closer to the truth than Julie was willing to admit. "He was a good father," she conceded.

"He was a lousy father, Julie; never at home,

never around when we needed him. Mother was left to do all the fathering when we were growing up.''

Julie realized that Emery, who had been their father's favorite, had seen him more clearly than she had. ''He always loved us.''

''Yes, he always loved us. But what about Noah, Julie? He does love you, you know. And he's a good man—every bit as good as Dad.''

''A good man in a bad profession.''

''When did you get so antiestablishment? You were always the conservative one in the family.''

Julie gave her a wry smile. ''I guess in the last few days.''

''Well, I think you should seriously consider becoming a part of it, Julie. And if you won't, then at least I think you ought to seriously consider Noah. He's a good man, and there aren't many of them out there. I should know.''

''So you're procuring for both the CIA and Noah. Well, the answer to both is no. I don't want to be a spy, nor do I want to live with a spy.''

''Oh, Noah's not really a spy. I think he does something like negotiate arms deals these days. His cover was blown years ago.''

''Then what was he doing—''

''Involved in this? Just helping out. He and Yotav are old friends.''

So it hadn't all been lies. Not that it made any real difference, but she was happy to hear he'd been straight about something. And negotiating arms was something she could conceivably live with.

''You know what I think?'' Julie asked her sister.

Emery's countenance brightened. "No, what?"

"I think we should order some dessert."

Emery laughed. "You order dessert, sweetie; I'm going to go find Yotav. One does not live by bread alone, Julie, in case you hadn't heard."

Julie not only had heard, she was in total agreement.

Chapter Fourteen

It was the sort of furnace day in New York City that might occur were the Sahara Desert and the tropics to form an alliance; the kind of day when people faint on the subways and kids open the fire hydrants to cool off in the spray, and classrooms in ghetto schools are pressure cookers ready to explode.

It was usual weather in August, but not so usual for September, but then Julie couldn't really complain. Her own classroom was suitably air-conditioned and if her students were going to explode, it would be out of boredom to judge by the faraway expressions on the faces before her.

No doubt they were thinking back to their vacations or ahead to what they'd do when the class was over and they were free to take to the streets and the park for the remainder of the day. Well, she wasn't thinking back if she could possibly avoid it, but she too was thinking ahead, in her case to her quiet apartment where she'd fix herself a glass of iced tea and then put tired feet up before contemplating the papers handed in by two prior classes.

"Dr. Domino!"

She looked up from her lecture notes on the podium to see a hand being waved above the seated heads. James Brunda again. Only two weeks into the new school year, and already he was determined to make his presence felt. He insisted on interrupting every lecture in Economic Theory with the kind of meaningless questions best left unanswered. She knew his real purpose was to make himself known to her, and in that he was succeeding all too well. A more tiresome student she couldn't imagine.

"Yes, Mr. Brunda, what is it?" Making it sound, she feared, like "What is it now?" At least she seemed to be getting less of young men making nuisances of themselves in class since she'd become a brunette.

He was well into the formation of his question when the bell rang and the rest of the students, not waiting to be dismissed, began to file out. Julie patiently heard him out, then walked out of the building with him, still answering his lengthy question. She half expected him to suggest continuing the discussion at a local coffee house, to which she would plead her usual excuse of work, but he surprised her by leaving her at the entrance of the park after pleading work of his own.

She shifted her briefcase to her other hand and started through the park in the direction of her building. Roller skaters vied with people walking dogs and students charging after wildly thrown frisbees. A jazz group was playing in one part of the park while every other student seemed to be carrying his own transistor radio, each tuned to a different station. And yet the cacophony of sounds was pleasant and she felt as happy as the students at being released from school. So far this year she wasn't deriving her usual pleasure out of teaching.

That this was due to Noah was dismaying. She hadn't thought she'd ever allow a man to disrupt her life, and perhaps disrupt was too strong a word for it. But the tingle of apprehension she had first experienced when he hadn't called or tried to get in touch with her after that last night in London, was now refining itself into a state of permanent unease. Memories of him invaded her mind at the least opportune moments: sometimes in the middle of a lecture, often in department meetings, always at night when sleep refused to come. These thoughts became a link to the unquiet world beneath the surface of her outwardly orderly life.

At first in London she thought he'd call, perhaps leave a message for her at the hotel desk. Once home, she was sure he'd write, make contact in some way, any way. She had not thought him a man to be so easily dissuaded.

Why should I care whether I ever hear from him again? she often asked herself, and the answer always came back: *Because I love him.*

She stopped at a white-coated vendor and bought herself a Chipwich ice cream sandwich, then watched in dismay as the second bite of the fast-melting entity turned out to be a miss and the chocolate dribbled down the front of her beige linen dress. It annoyed her to have given in to oral gratification to the tune of a three dollar cleaning bill. So much for impulse buying!

She saw she was making matters worse by rubbing at her dress with the paper napkin, as though chocolate ever conveniently disappeared, when she heard a familiar chuckle from a nearby bench. She looked up into Noah's eyes, so surprised she let the rest of the sandwich fall to the path. Noah, with his same badly cut hair, his same steady gray eyes, and wearing the white pants and navy shirt they had purchased together at Macy's.

She was so happy to see him she just stood there, unable to move or even to speak. Hitherto she hadn't, even in her most satisfying fantasies, credited him with the capability for making such a romantic gesture as just showing up, at the right time, in the right place.

He beckoned her over to the bench, at the same time saying, "Never mind, you're too old for ice cream in the park, anyway. I don't know about you, but I could use a drink."

"What are you doing here?" she asked him, still not quite believing her eyes or what her senses were telling her. Fantasies weren't supposed to really come true. "Don't tell me I'm being followed again."

He shook his head, his eyes warm as they locked with hers. "Not officially." Then he was standing in front of her, holding his arms out. "Give me a hug, Julie."

Not even caring who saw her, she moved in close to him, wrapping her arms around his broad back and resting her head on his shoulder.

"That feels good, Julie; that feels very good."

It did feel good, despite the fact it was much too hot out for such close physical contact. She took a step backwards and looked at him, noting the circles beneath his eyes, the drawn lines beside his mouth. "Oh, Noah—it's good to see you."

"I was hoping you'd say that. Does that mean I've been forgiven?" He tucked her arm through his and started to lead her back the way she had come.

"You're forgiven. In fact. . ."

He looked down at her. "In fact what?"

She chuckled. "I was just going to say that in fact my life's been a dead bore since I've been back."

"No kidding?"

She hugged his arm to her side. "No kidding. Don't get me wrong, though; I have no desire to emulate Emery."

"I wouldn't want you to. I had more in mind your emulating your parents."

She shot him a quizzical look, but he merely patted her arm. "I spotted a nice, quiet sidewalk café on the way here where we can get ourselves a cold drink and talk."

The nice, quiet sidewalk café turned out to be Le Figaro, and not so quiet, as by now it was filled with boisterous students who made it their hangout. Instead, Julie led him down the street to an Irish bar that for some reason didn't attract the students, and they sat across from each other in a wooden booth.

"I'd like a cold beer, light if they have it," she told Noah, who went to the bar and returned with two.

"How've you been, Julie?"

She accepted the proffered drink and took a long swallow before saying, "I've been fine. A little bored, as I said, but that'll pass."

"Did you stay on in London?"

"For a few days. Did some shopping, took a day trip to Oxford." She didn't add that it had been a bleak few days, that she'd missed him every minute.

"I was hoping you'd call me. I stuck around the embassy most of the day, but when I didn't hear from you, I flew back to Athens."

"I was too confused then, Noah."

"And since then?"

"Since then I've been getting ready for school. Anyway, you could've called me."

He grinned. "I did better than that; I showed up in person."

She took another sip of her beer, marveling that he was actually sitting across from her. She'd been certain she'd never see him again, and while she knew she wanted to see him once more, she doubted she'd ever have made the first move. Not that she hadn't considered it. She'd started numerous letters to him, but each time the result had ended up in her wastebasket, and she'd ended up more frustrated. When it had come right down to it, she hadn't known what to say.

"So what is this business of emulating my parents? Is it that you think I should be some combination lawyer/newscaster?"

He was shaking his head. "I wasn't thinking of their professions. What I was suggesting was that you get married."

Which, if it was a proposal, was decidedly ambiguous. "Well, Noah, it's not as though I'm a spinster schoolteacher out of choice." His unspoken question hovered between them like an unwanted third party. "I guess I just haven't met the right man," she added lamely.

"You've met him, Julie." He slid down in his seat and she felt his knee pressed up against hers. Just a silly thing like that was enough to make her shiver.

She drew in her breath. "Is this a proposal, Noah?"

"I told you in London I loved you, didn't I?"

"That's different. That is totally different. That is so totally irrelevant..."

"What was irrelevant about it?" A baffled look on his face.

"I'll tell you what was irrelevant about it, Noah. You lied to me about everything, so why should I have believed you that time?"

"If we're going to talk about lies, Julie—"

"Yes, let's talk about lies."

He took his time lighting a cigarette before answering her. "Well, let's just say that if we had a scale on the table here, and if we were to put your lies on one side, and mine on the other—your side would be hitting the table, Julie."

Enraged, she moved her knee out of the way of his. "But you knew I was lying, that's the difference. It was all part of your devious scheme."

"That's going to come back now to haunt me, is that it? Julie, just believe this: What was between us was never part of that devious scheme. And when I told you in London that I loved you, it was no lie."

She found herself somewhat mollified by his words. "Yes, you told me you loved me, then invited me to the beach."

"I figured once I got you in Greece I'd be able to keep you there."

She felt the tension fast draining out of the situation. "Circumstances in London weren't conducive to romance, I'm afraid."

"And circumstances now?" But she could see by the look on his face that he didn't need to ask, that he knew quite well how she was feeling.

Someone put money in the jukebox and loud rock poured out of the machine. "I just don't see how it's possible," she shouted over the music.

"What did you say?" he yelled back, then got up and moved over beside her in the booth. "What was that?" he repeated.

"I don't see how it's possible. You live in Greece and I live in New York. Unless you had some kind of long distance arrangement in mind."

His face was engulfed by a smile. "Is that a yes?"

"No, it's not. I just don't see how it could work."

"But you do love me, don't you?"

She leaned against him. "Of course I love you."

"That's fantastic! Wait here just a minute."

She watched as he made the trip to the bar, then returned with a bottle of champagne and two glasses.

"This calls for a celebration," he said, pouring them each a glassful.

"What are we celebrating?"

"For starters, the fact that you love me." He

touched her glass with his, said, "To us," then emptied the contents in one gulp. Julie drank somewhat less, not wanting to spoil the moment by telling him she didn't really like champagne, and allowed him to refill both glasses.

"So how soon can we leave for Athens?" he asked her, obviously assuming everything was settled.

"It's not that simple, Noah; I have a teaching contract."

"Break it."

"I can't do that. And anyway, what would I do in Greece?"

"I suppose you wouldn't consider just being my wife."

"You suppose right."

"There's universities there, Julie. A very good one right in Athens."

"Sure, but I don't happen to speak the language. And that's generally a prerequisite to teaching in a foreign country."

"I'll teach you."

"Oh, Noah, that would take years. Now maybe Italy..."

"Italy?"

"I'm fluent in Italian."

"That's great, but I'm afraid we don't negotiate arms with the Italians."

"It would be a lot easier if you'd get transferred to New York."

"To do what? Negotiate arms deals with the street gangs in the Bronx?"

"Couldn't you get a job with the UN?"

He shook his head. "I'm not a diplomat, Julie, I'm an arms negotiator."

It would seem they were at an impass. She couldn't break her teaching contract and retain her credibility in academic circles, but she also couldn't reasonably expect him to give up his job to accommodate her. Nor would she be willing to give up the profession it had taken her years of school to achieve.

"You could always consider working for the government," he was saying to her.

"As a spy?" Incredulous.

"Julie, even I wouldn't want my wife to be a spy."

"As an arms negotiator?"

"Why are you continuously putting words in my mouth? I had in mind as an economist."

"Even if they needed an economist and I qualified, there'd be no guarantee I'd be posted to Greece. In fact that would seem highly unlikely."

He shrugged. "Maybe I could pull a few strings."

"Why don't you pull a few strings for yourself and get into another field?"

"Because that's what I'm best at. And that's where I'm needed."

She moved her hand to his and took it, their fingers intertwining. "Even if it can't work out, Noah, I'm not sorry I met you. And I'll always remember—"

"Shut up, Julie!"

She dropped her hand. "What?"

"I said shut up. You were starting in on some final, farewell scene, and I don't want to hear it."

"I was only going to say—"

"I know what you were going to say. Some romantic drivel about how you'd never forget me, am I right?"

She sat in stony silence, a mulish look creeping across her face.

"Well, I can personally assure you you're never going to forget me, and that's because we're going to be together."

Somehow, during all her romantic daydreaming about him, she had neglected to remember how annoyingly supercillious he was capable of being. She shoved her champagne glass out of the way and took a drink of her beer before folding her arms across her chest and moving closer to the wall and farther away from him in the close confines of the booth. A booth that only moments ago had seemed cozy to her.

"Well, that's just romantic drivel on your part, Noah, because it just isn't going to be possible."

He shoved his own champagne glass out of the way, finished his beer, then stood up and held out his hand to her. "Come on, we're getting out of here."

"Where're we going?" Staying in place.

He reached down and pulled her out of the booth. "Back to your place. Listen, I didn't get a chance to change any money. . . ."

"You mean I'm paying for the champagne? I don't even like champagne."

He grinned. "Neither do I, but there are certain times in life when one is required to drink it."

"And this was one?"

"Damn right!"

She left enough money for the drinks, then followed him to the door. "Why're we going back to my place?"

He put one warm arm around her shoulders as they headed back to the park. "Because I want some privacy."

Shivers of anticipation began to run through her body. "Privacy for what?" she inquired, her voice as casual as she was capable of making it in view of the fact she was already anticipating the answer. Anticipating it and approving of it.

He stopped on the sidewalk and looked down at her. "For what I do best."

Her eyes lit up, and at the sight of them he burst out laughing. "No, not that, Julie; at least not for the moment. I'm grateful for the compliment, but this time we're going to do what I really do best—we're going to negotiate!"

WIN A CRUISE TO ROMANCE!
Enter the Harlequin Intrigue™** Sweepstakes.

Here's your chance to win a trip-for-two to the romantic Caribbean. A week of relaxing, sun-filled days and moonlit nights aboard the luxurious Cunard *Countess*.

And all you have to do is write in the name of the new Harlequin®* series in the top right-hand corner above. It's that easy! Be sure and send your entry before October 31, 1984.

No purchase necessary. Void where prohibited. Incomplete and incorrect entries still valid for drawing. See reverse for official rules.

SEND ENTRIES TO:

IN U.S.: Harlequin Cruise to Romance Sweepstakes, Suite 3395, 175 Fifth Avenue, New York, NY 10010

IN CANADA: Harlequin Cruise to Romance Sweepstakes, Suite 191, 238 Davenport Road, Toronto, Ontario M5R 1J6

NAME_____

ADDRESS_____

CITY_____ STATE/PROV._____

ZIP/POSTAL CODE_____ PHONE_____

INT-SW-2

Harlequin Cruise to Romance Sweepstakes
OFFICIAL RULES   NO PURCHASE NECESSARY

1. The **Harlequin Cruise to Romance Sweepstakes** is open to all residents of Canada (with the exception of the Province of Quebec) and the United States 18 years or older at the time of entry. Employees and their families of Harlequin Enterprises Limited, their affiliated companies, advertising/promotion agencies and RONALD SMILEY INC. also excluded.

2. To enter, complete the Official Entry form. It is not necessary to answer the questions on the entry to qualify. You may write the name of the new Harlequin series, Harlequin Intrigue, on a separate 3″ x 5″ piece of paper along with your full name and address, or on the entry form. Canadian residents mail each entry, one only to an envelope to: **Harlequin Cruise to Romance Sweepstakes, Suite 191, 238 Davenport Road, Toronto, Ontario M5R 1J6.** United States residents mail each entry, one to an envelope to: **Harlequin Cruise to Romance Sweepstakes, Suite 3395, 175 Fifth Avenue, New York, NY 10010.** All entries from Canada and the United States must be postmarked by the sweepstakes closing date of October 31, 1984, to be eligible. Not responsible for late, lost or misdirected mail.

3. Winners will be selected within 90 days after closing date in random drawings from among all valid Canadian and United States entries received by RONALD SMILEY INC., an independent judging organization whose decisions are final. Canadian residents whose entry may be randomly drawn must answer correctly a time-limited arithmetical skill-testing question in order to win the related prize. Major prize winner will be notified by registered mail and will be required to submit an Affidavit of Compliance within 14 days of notification. In the event of non-compliance or if any prize notifications are returned to Harlequin Enterprises Limited or Ronald Smiley Inc., alternate winner will be randomly selected and notified. Winner may be asked to use their name and photo at no additional compensation. Odds of winning depend on the number of all valid Canadian and United States entries received. No substitution, duplication or cash redemption of prizes. Any applicable taxes are the winner's responsibility. This offer will appear prior to closing date of October 31, 1984 in Harlequin Reader Service mailings, the August 1984 issues of *The Globe, People, National Examiner,* the September 1984 issues of *Good Housekeeping* and *Woman's Day,* and at participating retailers.

4. The following are the prizes to be awarded. One 7-day Cunard Caribbean Cruise for Two scheduled to depart and return from San Juan, Puerto Rico. Winner and guest will be provided round trip coach airline tickets from winner's nearest applicable airport to San Juan, Puerto Rico. Cruise prize includes 1 cabin for two and meals as served aboard. Cruise is scheduled to visit Tortola, Nevis, St. Kitts, Guadeloupe, St. Lucia, St. Maarten, St. Thomas and St. John. The cruise itinerary may be changed by cruise line. A cruise of same substance may be substituted by sponsor. Port taxes and any other expenses incurred by the winner and guest on the cruise boat or land is their responsibility. Cruise must be taken by June 30, 1985, subject to available dates. The approximate retail value of First Prize in United States dollars is $4,000/Canadian dollars is $4,900.00.

    100 Second Prizes will be awarded of a one-year subscription each to the Harlequin Reader Service for 24 Harlequin Intrigue publications. The approximate retail value of each Second Prize in United States dollars is $54.00/Canadian dollars is $60.00.

5. To receive a First Prize winner's list Canadian residents send a stamped, self-addressed envelope to: Harlequin Cruise to Romance Winner's List, Suite 323, 238 Davenport Road, Toronto, Ontario M5R 1J6. United States residents send a self-addressed, stamped envelope to: Harlequin Cruise to Romance Winner's List, Suite 3115, 175 Fifth Avenue, New York, NY 10010. Residents of Ohio only need not apply return postage. All requests must be postmarked by October 31, 1984, for response.

This sweepstakes offer in Canada is subject to all Federal, Provincial and Municipal laws and regulations and is void in the Province of Quebec and wherever prohibited by law. This offer in the United States is subject to all Federal, State and local laws and regulations and void wherever prohibited by law.

*Trademark of Harlequin Enterprises Limited.

Harlequin Stationery Offer